CURVES FOR THE DRAGON

A NOVEL BY

ANNABELLE WINTERS

Books by Annabelle Winters

The CURVES FOR SHEIKHS Series

Curves for the Sheikh
Flames for the Sheikh
Hostage for the Sheikh
Single for the Sheikh
Stockings for the Sheikh
Untouched for the Sheikh
Surrogate for the Sheikh
Stars for the Sheikh
Shelter for the Sheikh
Shared for the Sheikh
Assassin for the Sheikh
Privilege for the Sheikh
Ransomed for the Sheikh
Uncorked for the Sheikh
Haunted for the Sheikh
Grateful for the Sheikh
Mistletoe for the Sheikh
Fake for the Sheikh

The CURVES FOR SHIFTERS Series

Curves for the Dragon
Born for the Bear
Witch for the Wolf

CURVES FOR THE DRAGON

A NOVEL BY

ANNABELLE WINTERS

2019
RAINSHINE BOOKS
USA

Copyright Notice

CURVES FOR THE DRAGON

1
ATHRAAK PROVINCE
BORDER OF SYRIA AND IRAQ

Adam Drake closed one eye—the green one—and looked through the scope on his custom-built sniper rifle that had an extended range. He knew he wasn't going to take the shot, though. You don't kill a man without giving him a chance to fight back, a chance to surrender, a chance to bow down to your superiority, to beg for his goddamn life. You don't kill a man from a mile away. You do it up close, so he knows what's about to happen, understands that his own actions have led to this moment, led him to face Adam Drake, the Dragon of the Desert.

Say my name, whispered his dragon as Adam raised his head from the scope and looked out over the desert landscape. *Call me forth and we will fly there and take him. Burn him alive. Eat him whole, bones and everything. Hmmm, crunchy!*

"We are not eating anyone today," Adam muttered, shaking his head and blinking. He squinted into the distance, past the golden sand-dunes of the Athraaki desert, this lawless land somewhere between Syria and Iraq, a place where he'd lived in self-imposed exile for what seemed like too long now. "It doesn't help us when we eat our targets. We can't collect a bounty when there's no proof we finished the job."

We can save a couple of his teeth for identification, said his dragon, and Adam almost smiled at the thought of himself Changed into dragon form, becoming one with his daemon, all that fire and fury unleashed, burning everything in his path, eating flesh and crunching bone and then delicately placing two rear molars in a Ziploc bag to hand over to John Benson in the CIA so he could collect the bounty.

"I'm pretty sure our target doesn't have any dental records that can be used to match his teeth that you so generously offered not to eat. And who eats teeth, anyway?"

A monster, replied his dragon. *That is what we are, yes? A monster with green-and-gold wings, talons as thick* as pillars, sharp as spears, breathing fire and bringing vengeance to the wicked.

"Can we not be so goddamn dramatic, please?" Adam muttered, twisting the scope on his rifle and leaning in to get another look at the target amidst the small group of armed militants.

Why do you bother with that scope? Just say my name and you will have the power of my vision at your command. I can hunt a worm from a mile up in the sky.

"A worm? Isn't that like your cousin or something?"

Mock me all you want. You know I am you, and so you only mock yourself. Now say my name and give me control. We need to fly. We need to burn. We need to—

Adam gritted his teeth, cutting off his dragon's inner voice. It had been years since he'd gained control of the dragon inside, the dark side of his being, brought it under his command after almost losing himself to its unbridled power. Now the Change only happened at his command, when he called his dragon by name. But over the past few months he could feel a restlessness within him, a yearning that he knew only meant one thing, the most primal of needs, the need for a—

"What the hell?" Adam muttered as he glanced through the scope again, his body tensing up when he saw a caravan of ten SUVs and trucks rumble towards his target, a leader of an insurgent party. The man had a bounty on his head: $500,000 from the U.S. and another $250,000 from the United Kingdom. Not a bad score for a pretty easy target. But these new arrivals changed things. To handle this level of activity, he might need to . . . Change.

He felt his dragon stir as he had the thought, and Adam blinked as his vision blurred for a moment and then suddenly flipped to dragon-sight, that crisp, clear, ultrafocused vision that let him see miles beyond what even the most powerful military scope afforded. He felt his green eye move left, sensed his gold eye turn right, giving him that expanded field of view that was so damned useful in a fight.

"There isn't gonna be a fight today," Adam muttered as he surveyed the scene. "We aren't killing a hundred people just to collect a bounty on one guy. We'll keep eyes on him and take him down when there's a little less heat."

More heat, whispered his dragon. *More heat, Adam. Say my name. Say my goddamn name.*

Adam felt a catch in his throat as he felt his dragon try to take control. It surprised him, and for a moment he thought he might Change without giving the command, without calling forth his dragon by name.

He felt a sharp pain behind his left eye, and when he focused again he saw that some of the trucks had stopped, their canopies flipped open as the militants gathered around to examine its contents.

"Oh, shit," Adam muttered. "Hell, no."

But there was no mistaking what he was witnessing down there in the lawless desert: The trucks were filled with people. Women. Girls. Adam had heard rumblings about this: Insurgents kidnapping women from unprotected villages. Women that would become war-brides to insurgent leaders, sex-slaves to the foot-soldiers, property to be used, abused, and then discarded. He sighed and shook his head. There was no walking away now. Not after he'd seen this.

Slowly he stood up, unstrapping his equipment belt and tossing it into his Jeep along with the rifle. He wouldn't need the rifle. He wouldn't need any of this. He would just need to become who he was: That avenging angel. The Desert Dragon.

A moment later he'd pulled off his khaki shirt, dropped his trousers, and then he was buck naked under the desert sun. He looked down at his lean, hard, deeply tanned body and took a long breath as he visualized his line of approach, his method of attack.

Then he exhaled slowly and spoke the word.

He said the name.

He unleashed the beast.

2

MILWAUKEE, WISCONSIN
UNITED STATES

"**W**ait, what's the name again?"

"Adam Drake. Don't you remember him from high school?"

"Ohhh, yeah! The Bronze Beast, right? Didn't he go . . . I dunno . . . *crazy*?!"

Asheline Brown chuckled as she shook her head at her best friend Polly. The woman didn't have any filters—which was fine, because when it came to her work, Ash was all filters. She had to be, because being a serious journalist meant you needed to protect your sources with everything you had. That was the way you got to the big stories. And Adam Drake was a big story. Ash could feel it. She could almost smell it, it was so damned close!

"What's that smell?" Ash said, sniffing the air like an animal and frowning at Polly. Then her eyes went wide and she turned and made a mad dash for the kitchen. "You didn't turn off the oven, you moron!" she screamed just as the first thick plume of black smoke came swirling around the corner to greet her.

"Was I supposed to? You just told me to take the stuff out because it was done. Oh, shit, I'm so, so sorry! I'm calling 911! Hold on!"

"Don't call 911. I got this," Ash said calmly, squinting through the smoke as she pulled open the cabinet above the stove and grabbed her spray bottle with a special concoction of baking soda. She pulled open the oven, blasted her home-made potion into it, and then slammed the oven-door closed and ran to open the windows.

In minutes the smoke had made its way out of the kitchen, and Ash sighed and placed her hands on her wide hips, pinching her own love-handles as she glared at Polly and then glanced over at the home-made bear-claws sitting patiently on the counter.

"Good job," she said to Polly, smiling at the perfectly shaped pastries. "Just some frosting, and then lunchtime!"

Polly was still breathing heavily as she stared at Ash, then the bear-claws, and finally back up at Ash. "Good job? Lunchtime?! Ash, I almost burned down your house!" She frowned and looked up at the ceiling. "I can't believe the smoke alarm didn't go off."

Ash winked and pulled open one of the drawers. In it was a smoke-alarm, disabled, dismantled, and possibly broken. "I don't need a smoke alarm. The sound drives me insane. Besides, I have a really good sense of smell, especially when something's on fire."

Polly shook her head as she finally calmed down enough to look at the tray of pastries that was going to be their Sunday lunch. They did this every Sunday, the two of them. Bear-claws with extra frosting, and then Netflix until their eyes bugged out.

"Speaking of insane," she said as Ash pulled out a massive tube of red frosting. Always red. "Why were we talking about Adam Drake anyway?"

"So you remember him," Ash said, blinking at the memory of that intense, smoldering hot . . . beast. The bronze beast. They'd called him that because he was always tanned, even in the dead of the Wisconsin winter, when there'd been no sun for weeks! Once, some of the guys had teased him about going to a tanning salon like a pretty-boy. That was the only time anyone messed with Adam Drake. Ash didn't even want to think about that day when Adam Drake had taken on five or six guys in the schoolyard, breaking noses and knocking out teeth like a goddamn lunatic. No one saw Adam after that. Everyone assumed he'd been expelled or sent to some kind of juvenile rehab center.

"Yes, I remember him," said Polly, dipping her pinky into the red frosting and tasting it. "Voted Most Likely to become a Psycho Killer. Is that what this is about? He finally went full-on nuts and killed someone? Is that the story?"

"Something like that," Ash said, taking a breath as she put the final squeeze on their sugary lunch and stepped back to admire her work. Bear-claws. Always bear-claws with blood-red frosting. "But no, one of my sources mentioned his name the other day. So I looked him up, and it turned out he joined the military after high-school. Actually he never finished high-school, but whatever."

Polly rolled her eyes. "Well, that backs up my suspicion that the military is full of psychos who just want an excuse to kill someone."

Ash whipped her head around, the anger rising so fast she had to clench her fists and jaw at the same time just to stay in control. "Don't you dare badmouth the military in my presence! These men and women risk their lives so we can live fat and happy, all right? Got it?"

Polly took two steps back, her eyes going wide before she blinked three times. "Whoa! Shit, I'm sorry, babe! I forgot about your parents for a moment. And your brother, ohmygod! I . . . I . . ."

"Let's just eat, OK?" Ash said, frowning as she looked down at her clenched fists. Yeah, the military was a hot-button for Ash after her parents, who worked for the Department of Defense, were killed when she was seven. Then her Army Ranger brother had gone MIA, his body never recovered, his death neither confirmed nor denied. It had driven her to become a journalist, to spend her career developing sources deep in the military and government—sources with whom she played a delicate game of give-and-take, sometimes writing stories that would serve their interests, other times respecting their wishes to hold back information that she felt the American people needed to know. She'd made compromises, but mostly her conscience was clear. She'd always felt like she was working towards something big, something that would change everything, something that would change *her*!

Change me into what, she wondered as she picked up two bear-claws and held them up to the light. The red frosting looked like blood, and Ash stared at her own hands as her vision blurred. She caught flashes of images, images that had been coming through in dreams over the past few months, images of herself as an animal, with claws and teeth, out-of-control, driven by raw instinct, a primal need, the need to run free, the need to roar wild, the need to . . . mate?

Ash closed her eyes tight and shook her head. Freakin' hormones, she told herself as she felt those telltale cramps coming on. Her periods over the past few months had been excruciating, with headaches so splitting she could barely handle them—and Ash could handle a lot!

"You all right, hon?" Polly said, putting down her bear-claw and touching Ash on the arm.

"What?" Ash said, her eyes flickering open, her mind returning to reality. "Oh, yeah. I'm fine. Maybe just the smoke. Let's head out to the porch."

"The porch? Um, it's December in Wisconsin, Ash. It's like two degrees outside."

"There's blankets near the door," Ash said simply. Suddenly she wanted the cold. She needed it. "Don't wipe your sticky fingers on them."

"I'll wipe my sticky fingers on *you* for subjecting me to this," Polly grumbled as she put one bear-claw on a plate and strutted her skinny butt towards the door. "I don't have the insulation you do, remember."

Ash opened her mouth wide as she stared at her waiflike friend. But then she just smiled and shook her head. Polly could get away with a remark like that. And anyway, Ash didn't care. She'd been a larger woman her entire life, and even back when she was just growing into her body, she was mostly comfortable with her curves no matter what anyone else said.

They sank into the oversized, all-weather chairs on the back-porch of the house. The house was with-

in Milwaukee city limits, so there wasn't much of a
backyard, and Ash sighed as she stared at the fence
dividing her property from the next. She'd grown up
in this house, and it had always seemed big enough,
even when it was a family of four. But now she felt
almost claustrophobic, caged, chained, restrained . .
. like she needed more space, space to roam, to run,
to be . . . herself. Her real self.

"Really?" came Polly's voice through Ash's roaming imagination.

"Really what?"

"Did Adam Drake really join the Army?

"Looks like he joined the Air Force, actually," said
Ash, her focus returning as she ate her first bear-claw
in three bites and let the sugar take over her system
in the most decadent way. "He did always have really good eyesight, if I remember correctly. There was
this one time he saw a penny on the sidewalk . . . the
sidewalk across the street! He ran through traffic to
grab it like it was treasure!"

Polly laughed. "Yeah, I remember that! He'd do
that all the time! Picking up coins and things from
the schoolyard! Weird."

Ash shrugged. "I guess he just liked money. Or maybe he was a hoarder in the making. Well, anyway, so
the best I could tell, he joined the Air Force, was selected to fly F-16 fighter jets."

"Wow, that's big deal, isn't it?"

"Yup," said Ash almost proudly. "But then there

were no more records of him. Couldn't find anything on him beyond four years in the Air Force. Not even from my regular sources in the military."

"Which means . . . what? He went crazy and they fired him? Or put him in military prison?"

"Well, no. If he was court-martialed or dishonorably discharged or quit or whatever, there'd be a record. In my experience, disappearing from the records means just one thing. Special Forces."

Polly's eyes widened and she stopped chewing, pulling her blanket closer around her thin shoulders. "Wow! Like the Navy Seals?"

Ash shrugged. She didn't stop chewing. Two bear-claws down, and she was just getting started. "Well, it would be Delta Force since he was a fly-boy. That's the Air Force's Special Ops group. They're serious guys. But still, there would be a record even if he was recruited into Delta Force; which means . . ." She trailed off as she connected the dots. They only led to one place, and she knew she should shut up.

"Means . . . *what*?" said Polly. "You can't leave me hangin' like this, you bitch!"

Ash snorted and took another bite and then another breath. "Black ops," she said quietly.

"Which is what? Like undercover stuff or something?"

Ash nodded. "Something like that. It's don't ask, don't tell stuff. Unofficial military missions. Stuff that the government would deny if those guys were ever caught, captured, or killed." She swallowed hard and blinked. "And most of the folks doing Black Ops are eventually killed."

"So maybe Adam's dead," Polly said with a shrug that annoyed Ash for some reason. Again she felt that strange sense of connection, even ownership, with Adam Drake, a weirdo she hadn't seen in over a decade.

"He's not dead," she said sharply. "He's doing something big, and I'm going to find out what it is. I'm going to break the story. Break it wide open."

3

Broken, Adam thought as he blinked himself back into focus and surveyed the scene. I'm broken again. I thought I had fixed this, but clearly I haven't. My dragon isn't under my control. Perhaps it never was. Perhaps I've been kidding myself.

He waited for his dragon to respond, but there was nothing but silence. He could feel the beast lurking within him, just behind his consciousness. But it was calm—more calm than he was!

"Because you got what you want, didn't you?" he whispered out loud as he looked over the scene. "You burned, killed, destroyed. Scorched the Earth and everything on it."

Around him were the charred remains of men's bodies, some of them half-eaten. Adam knew there had been more, but they'd been eaten by the beast, bones and all, crunched and swallowed whole like a scene from the Book of Revelation. His own memory of what had happened was hazy, and this troubled Adam as much as the carnage he'd unleashed by letting his dragon come out.

Because for years now, ever since he'd gained control of his dragon, controlled the Change, *commanded* the Change, Adam had been fully focused and alert when in dragon form. He always knew what he was doing, and those times were glorious: Stretching his massive green-and-gold wings, digging his talons into the Earth and pushing off into the skies, soaring above the clouds, to where the air was so thin that even planes couldn't stay up. But now something was unraveling. His dragon was slipping out of his control again. And that was bad. Bad for Adam, and worse for the world.

A chill went over him as he walked through the remains of the militants' caravan of trucks and jeeps. He felt like the last man on Earth on the day of the Apocalypse, naked and glistening with sweat as he stepped through burning metal and the ashes of everything else. His dragon's flame had been so hot even the guns were half-melted and twisted, and Adam shrugged and tried to tell himself that at least no one else would be able to use those instruments of death.

You are an instrument of death, he told himself angrily as he felt the coils of his dragon briefly clench as if it agreed with him and was happy about being called an instrument of death. The military was right to cut off all official contact with you. The military cares about control, and you can't even control yourself, so what hope did they have of controlling you?

"Surprised they haven't killed us yet," Adam said, exhaling when he saw the fresh tire-tracks of the largest truck—the truck with the kidnapped women. For a moment he'd been afraid that his dragon had burned even the ones they'd swooped in to save. But clearly they'd gotten away. Hopefully one of the women had taken the wheel and driven the rest of the girls off to safety, or else all of this would have been for nothing!

A hundred fewer militants is not nothing, whispered his dragon. *And the women got away. Do you not remember?*

Adam blinked as suddenly the memory came back clear as the desert sky: He'd flown in, his wings spread wide, eyes like burning slits as the militants screamed in horror and began to pepper the beast with bullets. Of course, the bullets simply bounced off his rock-hard scales, some of them ricocheting right back at the clusters of petrified men. He'd burned the first Jeep immediately, the one with a back-mounted machine gun that probably wouldn't have done any real damage but would have certainly been very loud and annoying. Then he'd gone straight for the truck with the women, turning in the air with breathtaking skill, driving one long talon right through the windshield—and through the driver's heart.

The other driver had flung open the door and tumbled out, screaming in Arabic as he raced through the desert. The dragon had set him aflame with a laser-focused blast of white-hot fire, and the man had flopped down face-first into the burning sand.

Then the dragon had landed in front of the truck of terrified women, spreading its wings protectively as it stared in with its burning eyes, one gold and the other green.

"Go," the dragon had hissed, and it was Adam's voice coming through the dragon—deeper and with a rumble that made the ground shake, but still Adam's voice. "Go home. You are free. Go home to your families. To your fathers, mothers, brothers. To your husbands and lovers, your boyfriends and mates. Love them. Cherish them. Make babies with them."

"Make *babies* with them?" Adam said, almost laughing as he watched his dragon-memories. "These women think we're the goddamn devil, and you tell them to go make *babies*?! What were you thinking, you goddamn freak?"

I was not thinking, replied the dragon. *It was a spur of the moment thing. An improvised speech.*

"You were not thinking. Exactly. From now on, let me do the thinking—*and* the speechwriting," Adam muttered as he remembered how one of the women, a larger woman with strong eyes, finally summoned up the courage to climb into the driver's seat and put the truck in gear. The truck hurtled over the dunes, the dragon shielding them with his wings and body until they were out of range.

And then the dragon turned back to the enemy, and Adam's memory went blank again.

He sighed and shook his head, looking around for his clothes. The fragmented memories meant that the dragon had completely taken over, was all beast at the time—all beast and zero human. It had done what came naturally to it: Burned, and fed. Those were instincts rooted deep in dragonblood, and although Adam could control it, there was no stopping it. Not now, not ever. You don't stop nature. You don't stop life.

Adam put his hands on his hips and glanced up into the sky, directly at the sun. The sun didn't bother his eyes. It gave him energy. He was fire just like the sun, and he grinned when he remembered that in the end he *had* called forth his dragon. He *had*said its name, given the command, set it loose.

"Well, so much for keeping a low profile," Adam grunted as he trudged back towards where he'd left his clothes and equipment. But then he realized that it was miles away, since he'd Changed and just flown here. Shit.

He glanced around again, took a deep breath, and then he was dragon once more, wings bursting from his broad, tattooed back, powerful haunches pushing off against the packed sand, sending up a cloud of gold dust as he took to the skies and flew back to his Jeep. It took only a few seconds, but in those few seconds Adam experienced that joy once again, that perfect union of the two sides of himself, man and beast, just the two of them beneath the burning sun, free and alive!

Alive . . . but alone, Adam thought as he landed by his Jeep and drew his wings back, the Change coming instantly as he gave the command in his mind. Alone in the world. Alone forever.

Not for long, whispered his dragon as Adam pulled his clothes back on and tossed his equipment back into his Jeep.

"What do you mean?"

She is coming.

"Who is coming?"

She is waking up.

"Who is waking up? And from what?" said Adam, a chill running along his muscled back as he slid into the driver's seat and glanced at his satellite phone. It was blinking, and a strange feeling of synchronicity took over his mind as he tapped on the phone and saw that it was an email message. An email message on a mostly dormant email account: His old email address that he'd kept active since high-school. He'd never understood *why* he'd kept the address—no one ever used it, and it was so dead that he didn't even get spam messages! But now there was a message.

Subject: Is this Adam Drake?

From: Asheline Brown

Message: You probably don't remember me, but I heard your name recently and thought I'd look you up. This is the only email address I could find for you, so fingers crossed! (Why aren't you on Facebook, btw?) We were in high-school together back in Milwaukee P.S. 69. (Public School 69—we never got sick of that joke, right?) Anyway, like I said, someone mentioned your name, and I thought it might be fun to catch up. We always wondered what happened to you. I know you joined the Air Force, and since my brother and I were Army brats, I'd love to hear some military stories—even if you are just a Flyboy.

Best wishes and hope to see you soon,

-Ash.

Adam stared at the email, frowning as an image of

Asheline Brown came roaring into his mind's eye clear as the moon on a desert night. He hadn't interacted with her much in high school—hell, he hadn't interacted with anyone much in high school! There was so much going on inside him back then that it was all he could do to handle himself! But he did remember Ash Brown. Even as a teenager she had curves that stood out, and he remembered thinking more than once that she was going to be a beautiful woman. All woman. All . . . his?

Inside him the dragon rumbled, and Adam swore it was a chuckle that the beast had just emitted.

Babies, whispered the dragon, the beast coiling inside him and then shuddering like it was laughing. *We are going to make babies. Little dragon babies. Or whatever kind of babies emerge from the coupling.*

"What the hell does that mean?" Adam said, scanning through the rest of the email and tossing the phone into the passenger seat. The empty passenger seat. Empty for far too long.

Coupling? It is a respectful term for—

"Shut up, you oaf," said Adam, shaking his head as a smile grew on his face. He knew what the beast was taking about. A mate. *His* mate. His fated mate. A woman who could stand by his side, as an equal, provide balance to the man and the beast. He'd heard about the concept from one of the few other shifters he'd known: A bear-shifter named Bartholomew. Bart and Adam—along with a quiet but deadly wolf shifter named Caleb—had been put together on that secret Black Ops squad, but both the operation and Bart had gone off the rails on that disastrous mission in South America. Bart had lost control of his bear and disappeared into the rainforest. The government had shut down the entire thing after that. Caleb disappeared—probably "shut down" by the government. In fact Adam was certain they would have tried to shut him and his dragon down too—if they could figure out how!

In the end they'd let Adam disappear to the wild Middle Eastern desert, mostly thanks to the intervention of a man named John Benson, a forward-thinking CIA man who had deep connections in almost every government in the free and not-so-free world. Benson, a man who always seemed to know more than he let on. A man with secrets, but a man that Adam somehow trusted. He'd come on the scene like it was fate.

Fate?

Just like this email?

"Fated mates are a myth," Adam said as he turned the key in the ignition. But there was no response. The Jeep was dead.

Then why have we not taken a mate . . . not taken a

*mate EVER?*responded the dragon. *What are you waiting for if not the fated one to arrive, for her to wake up to herself, to accept her true nature?*

"You know why I have not taken a mate," Adam said, his anger rising as he turned the key again and narrowed his eyes. "You remember what happened the last time? I almost killed the woman! The poor thing! There is no one who can handle me! Handle *us*! Now why the hell won't this goddamn piece of shit *start*?!"

The dragon was silent, and Adam slammed his hands against the wheel and sat back on the leather seat. This was a new Jeep. The gas tank was full. There was no reason why it shouldn't start.

No reason except fate, whispered the dragon. *You must go to her. Fly to her.*

"*Fly* to her? From Arabia to Wisconsin? Leave the beautiful burning desert for that frozen wasteland in the American Midwest? *You* are asking me to fly to Wisconsin in the middle of winter? God-damn I must be hard up," Adam muttered, half-smiling as he gave up on the Jeep and stared up into the clear blue skies. "Fly to Wisconsin, huh? For . . . for a date?"

A date with fate, chuckled the dragon as Adam clambered out of the Jeep. *A date with our mate!*

"Now you're a goddamn poet," Adam said. He sighed and thought for a moment. Then he just shrugged and shook his head. What the hell, he thought. This

Jeep is broken anyway. And I'm in the mood for a nice long flight. Yeah, what the hell.

He said the name, not even bothering to take his clothes off. Instantly the Change came, and Adam roared in exhilaration as his dragon burst through, his wings ripping out of his back, clothes shredded in an instant.

Then he was in the air, and after a quick circle Adam twisted back and swooped low over his Jeep, opening his throat and sending a stream of blue fire into the vehicle and grinning with razor-sharp teeth the size of a backyard fence as his brand new Jeep exploded in a ball of fire.

"This is why I have to keep buying new Jeeps," Adam shouted as he circled once more to make sure all traces of him were gone. Two flaps of his mighty wings and he was so high in the air that he swore he could see the whole world before him, perhaps the entire universe, time itself maybe: past, present, and future. Was it all the same? Was all of it meant to be? Destiny? Fate?

A date with fate, chuckled the dragon as they headed West, almost scaring a flock of African swallows into dropping dead. *Adam's got a date with fate!*

4

"It is *not* a date," Ash said firmly as she patted down the front of her black blouse, wondering if she should tuck it in. No. Her belly looked fat that way. Almost pregnant. Why did she eat that extra bear-claw yesterday?

Because I didn't expect him to reply so soon—or at all, she thought as she turned and checked her ass in the mirror. It looked bigger than usual. Was it the jeans? Should she go with something else? Nope. No hiding that ass.

"What did his email say?" Polly asked, raising an eyebrow as she glanced at Ash's butt and then down at her shoes.

"He just said OK," said Ash. "OK, and see you to-morrow. That was it. How do I look?"

"You look fabulous. It's definitely a date if he replied so soon. Where are you meeting?"

"Bosco's Coffee and Cake. Should I wear a hat? I don't want to wear a hat."

"Don't wear a hat. You have great hair. Bosco's brings back some memories. They still have those faux-leather booths?"

"Yup," said Ash. "Perfect for an interview. Which is what this is. Not a date."

"You've said that like ten times, which means it's definitely a date. Besides, does he *know* it's an interview?"

"The best interviews happen when the subject doesn't think it's an interview," said Ash, narrowing her brown eyes at her reflection and sucking in her round, rosy-red cheeks. She glanced at Polly for a moment, almost envying her friend for being effortlessly thin. She adjusted the underwire of her bra, frowning as she wondered why it felt so tight around her boobs. Was she actually getting fatter? Why did her bra feel so tight?

"Want me to drive you?" said Polly.

"Um, I have a truck. Why would I want you to drive me?"

Polly just shrugged, looking away and touching her neck.

"Ohmygod, you want to see Adam, don't you? You want to see what he looks like now?"

Polly shrugged again, her face going red. "Military weirdo. Special Forces. Bad-ass bad boy who fought everyone in high-school? Sounds hot." Now she was bright red. "And you said it wasn't a date, right? Just business, right?"

Ash felt herself turn red, but it wasn't embarrassment. She was actually . . . what, *jealous*?! Ridiculous! Where was that coming from, that almost possessive feeling about a man she hadn't seen in a decade, a man who'd been a wild boy when she'd last known him—*barely* known him at that!

"Don't you have a boyfriend?" Ash said, raising an eyebrow as her mouth twisted up. "A boyfriend that you won't let me meet yet. Which is very suspicious, by the way."

"You'll meet him soon enough," Polly said, blinking and looking away. "All right. So I guess I'm not driving you?"

Ash sighed. "No, you can drive me. Come on. He's probably there by now. It's unprofessional to be late."

5

"**S**orry I'm late," Ash said, walking briskly into Bo-sco's, hand outstretched as she headed for Adam Drake.

She'd recognized him immediately. He'd barely changed—in fact only his eyes gave away the fact that he'd aged since high school. His skin was smooth and clear, bronze as always, his features cut and chiseled in a way that reminded her that the man was devas-tatingly handsome. And those eyes . . . God, she re-membered those eyes now! One green and one gold, like a surrealist painting!

"Adam, right? Adam Drake?" she said when the man didn't reply. He was just sitting there at a four-person table in the center of the coffee-shop, staring at her like he'd seen a ghost or perhaps like he didn't see her at all. "Thanks for getting a table, but can we move to a booth? I like the booths. Much easier to have a conversation. You remember this place from high-school? It's changed, but they kept the booths." She had to stop just to take a breath, she was talking so fast. Then she realized Adam hadn't said a word. "Hello?" she said. "Anyone home? I'm Ash! Ta-daa!"

She held her arms out and forced a smile, but the self-consciousness was rising in her and suddenly her tight bra felt like it was suffocating her. In fact, *all* her clothes felt really freakin' tight now, and she frowned as she felt the tiny hairs on the back of her neck stand up at attention, as if they were just waking up, just coming alive, coming forth . . .

And then suddenly Adam stood up, his mismatched eyes going wide and then rolling up in his head as if he was having a seizure. She stared as he spread his arms out wide, and then her mouth hung open at what came next:

Wings. Bursting out of his back. Green and gold wings tearing through his sweater as the veins on his thick neck bulged like they were going to pop. She could feel the heat rise in the room, hear the other customers screaming, knocking down tables and chairs as they scrambled to get out of the way! Bosco himself had fled the scene, and suddenly it was just Ash and Adam . . . well, Ash and whatever the hell *this* was!

"Oh. My. God," she heard herself say as she watched Adam writhe and flail like he was struggling, fighting against some creature that lived inside him and was trying to get out. It felt like a scene from a teen horror flick, but for some reason Ash wasn't horrified. She was fascinated. Transfixed.

Transformed.

"Get. Out," Adam shouted, the words coming out strained, his voice so deep that she swore she felt the tiles shake beneath her feet. "Now! I can't hold it back. I can't stop the Change. I can't—"

The rest of his words were swallowed up by a sound she'd never heard before, a deep, rumbling, throaty growl, the sound of a beast that was not of this world—not the world she knew, anyway.

And then those wings burst through all the way, crashing into the far sides of the walls, smashing through brick like it was nothing, cracking concrete like it was cardboard. Ash's eyes went even wider as she watched Adam Drake expand somehow, his clothes falling away as iridescent scales rippled up through his skin, gigantic talons slid out through his outstretched arms.

The heat was almost unbearable, and Ash could feel plaster falling from the ceiling as Adam's head blasted up against it. Or at least it *used* to be Adam's head. Now it was the head of a beast, a demon, a . . . a *dragon*?!

"Oh, God, this isn't happening," Ash muttered as she felt her world begin to close in on her. She thought she was going to be sick, and although a part of her knew that the entire building was going to collapse as this beast flapped its mighty wings and smashed walls, broke brick, destroyed concrete, she still couldn't move. "Oh, God, I—"

Suddenly a big piece of plaster landed on her head, and Ash stumbled and then swooned, her vision going blurry, the shaking floor coming up to meet her as she fell.

But she didn't fall, and the last thing she saw before blacking out was a mighty claw with shining talons wrap itself around her waist and lift her, lift her up as the beast smashed through the facade of the devastated building and took to the skies.

6

Adam was already soaring above the city of Milwaukee when he realized what had happened. Something that hadn't happened in years. Something he thought could never happen. His dragon had come forth without the command, without him calling its name! He'd been unable to stop the Change! He'd lost control! No! *No*! All that effort, all those years of loneliness, roaming the barren desert as he struggled to control what was inside him, to control the unbridled power of the dragon, the raw instinct that was a part of him, whether he liked it or not.

He glanced down at the woman in his talons, and he saw that her teeth were chattering, her lips turning blue. Shit, they were high in the sky in the middle of a Wisconsin winter! She was freezing to death!

Adam glanced down to see if he could land anytime soon. But it was all houses below him. There was no building big enough to hold him, and he wasn't sure if he could Change back. Even if he did, he'd be naked, with a passed out, half-frozen woman in his arms!

Use our heat, whispered the dragon as Adam stared down at Ash. *She will not burn.*

"What? Everything burns," Adam shot back as he glided aimlessly above the city. There were fields in the distance, but no shelter. Nothing warm. No heat except for . . .

And then his jaw opened wide and he was breathing his fire, enveloping Ash in golden flame, his panic rising as he wondered if he was killing her, turning Ash to . . . ash.

But his dragon was right, and Ash opened her eyes and smacked her lips as the color came rushing back to her face. She blinked up at him, her brown eyes going wide as she looked upon his hideous face, the face of a monster, the visage of a beast, the eyes of a . . .

"Dragon," she whispered. "Ohmygod, you're a dragon! Adam Drake is a dragon! What a story! What a scoop! I'll win the Pulitzer for this! Just gotta reach my notepad. Just gotta . . ."

And then she passed out in his arms, a smile on her red lips, her body going limp as the dragon blanketed her with fire, flapped his gold-and-green wings, and wondered what the hell was happening here.

7

Adam turned away from her. She was still passed out, but her breathing was slow and steady, her bosom rising and falling in perfect rhythm. Adam could hear her heart beat like it was a drum inside his goddamn head, and he blinked and stared at the dark walls of the abandoned barn.

He knew this place. It was a few miles from where he'd lived during his time in America. It was an abandoned farm that was owned by some farming company or something. Perhaps the land was fallow or they'd just forgotten they owned it, and so Adam had decided it was his. He liked the massive old barn. This was where he'd first Changed. This was where he'd first learned of who he was . . . of *what* he was.

But what is *she*, he wondered as he turned toward her again, averting his eyes from her naked body even though a part of him desperately wanted to look, to take in the sight of her smooth curves, her beautiful breasts, her thick thighs, that dark triangle daintily nestled between her legs.

So you did look, his dragon said. *Good. At least you are not made of stone. No need to feel guilty. You will be seeing a lot of her without her clothes.*

"I did not *look*," Adam said through gritted teeth as he scanned the empty barn for something to cover her with. It wouldn't do to have her wake up, find herself naked, and think that he . . . no. Absolutely not. "Her clothes were burned off, and I happened to glance at her as I put her down. I wasn't *looking*. I just happened to see." Adam finally saw a bale of hay that looked reasonably clean. He had no idea how old it was, but hey, it was . . . hay. Dried grass. It wasn't getting any deader.

And she will die of cold if you don't cover her. And if you don't figure out what to do with her pretty damned soon, Adam thought as he hastily dumped the hay over her, taking care not to stare at her while she was passed out and vulnerable. He might be a monster, but he was also a gentleman.

You know that our thoughts are one, said the dragon almost smugly. *You can pretend to be a gentleman, but we both know what you want. What we want. What she wants. Wake her up and take her. She is yours.*

"Enough with that fated mates bullshit," Adam said, stepping back from the pile of hay beneath which Ash Brown lay still as if in a coma. "Nobody is taking anyone. Not yet, at least." He frowned as he looked down at himself. Shit, he was naked too. During planned Changes, he often carried a backpack with clothes for when he Changed back. But this hadn't been a planned Change, and a chill went up Adam's back when he realized that about forty people had seen him turn into a goddamn dragon at Bosco's Coffee and Cake in downtown Milwaukee! It was probably all over the Internet by now! "And what the *hell* was that?! Are you trying to get us killed?"

I am trying to get us mated, said the dragon. *You were taking too long.*

"Too long? Too *long*?!" Adam shouted. "She'd just walked into the place! She'd barely said two words!"

And you had barely said a word. Anyway, I do not have patience for idle chitchat. When I see my mate, I take her. That is what dragons do. That is what we do.

"Well, we are part-human too, and humans do not just *take* their mates in the middle of coffee shops. At least not until after some idle chitchat. And anyway, she is a human. We cannot mate with a human while in dragon form. We would kill her. What were you thinking?"

I do not think. I just do. I am not the brains of this operation. I fly, burn, destroy, and mate.

"Goddamn animal," Adam muttered as he began to pace, taking long strides as he shook his head and clenched his fists. He knew he was just talking to himself, that the dragon was a part of him, it *was* him. Yes, it was the dumb, unthinking part of him, but his dragon also gave him access to the ancient wisdom that was buried in his subconscious, written in the stars, decreed by the Gods. He'd learned to trust that old wisdom, even when it came through the smug whispers of his resident beast.

And now the beast was saying that this woman was his mate! His fated mate! Could it be? Did he feel it? What would it feel like? Wouldn't he know it if she was?

"Why didn't she burn?" Adam asked, frowning as he stood above Ash and folded his arms, feeling his biceps go tight, his abs clench, his buttocks and thighs strain as a strange energy passed through him. He glanced down at himself, blinking in astonishment when he saw that he was erect like a post, his thick cock filled out and sticking straight ahead, pointing straight at Ash Brown like she was the goddamn North Star! "Oh, shit," he muttered, putting his hands on his hips as he wondered what the hell to do. Could he leave her here, fly out to the city, and pick up some clothes? But how? He had no wallet. No money.

But he did have a wallet earlier, didn't he? Shit, yes. He kept lockboxes all over the world with IDs, cards, and cash, and he'd visited the one at the Milwaukee Post Office before his "date." Of course, when his dragon had broken through at Bosco's, he'd ripped his way through his clothes. Which meant that somewhere in the rubble of Bosco's Coffee and Cake was his wallet—complete with credit cards and ID! Yeah, it was one of his many fake identities, but it had his real photograph on it! If that photograph got scanned into a government database with facial-recognition software . . .

"Shit," Adam said, shaking his head as the thoughts came rolling in with the fury of a firestorm. "Once the news hits that some kind of dragon-man was seen, and if my photograph shows up in the rubble, they'll know I'm alive. And then even John Benson might not be able to protect me. No. No goddamn way. You dumb beast! Dumb. Dumb. *Dumb!*"

Adam was furious, his head shaking as he clenched his jaw. His hands were still on his tight hips, his feet planted squarely on the ground, his cock still sticking straight out like it had a mind of its own, like nothing was under Adam's control anymore.

Then he heard something come through his swirling mind, and it took a moment for him to realize it was coming from down by his feet. It was a muffled sound, like nothing on Earth.

"Ohmygod!" came the muffled sound, and Adam's eyes went into full focus when he realized Ash was awake and alert, staring directly up at him as he stood over her, naked and bronze, his cock still sticking out like a tree-trunk leaning out over a river. "Oh. My. *God*!"

8

Oh. My. *God*!

Ash kicked out with her legs, coughing and sputtering, spitting out bits of hay as she screamed and tried to stand. She'd regained consciousness just in time to see Adam Drake standing above her, naked like an animal, muscled like a beast, veins rippling all over his hard body . . . with something else hard, muscled, and beastly sticking straight out, thick and heavy like a goddamn log.

"Leave me alone, you beast!" she screamed, still coughing up hay as she crawled away from him as fast as she could, on her hands and knees. Then she felt the burn of the cold ground on her knees, and she looked down at herself and saw her boobs swinging naked and free. "What the *hell*?!" she screamed, turning towards him and glaring as the rage kicked out any fear she had of this animal. "What did you do? Why am I . . . oh, my God. You didn't. You—"

"Of course I didn't!" he said, his eyes going wide. He came towards her, his cock bouncing as he walked, his balls swinging free in all their glory. "I'm a gentleman!"

"A gentleman who stripped me naked while I was passed out?" Ash shouted, covering her boobs with one arm and placing her other hand squarely over her pussy.

"Well, I burned your clothes, and so—"

"You *burned* my clothes? That was a new sweater!"

Adam blinked at her, and Ash could see him swallowing hard. "Well, it was a very nice sweater," he said, his eyes narrowing as a half-smile came to his dark red lips.

Ash was taken aback, and she blinked too, forcing back a smile as she reminded herself that she was furious, angry, mad as hell. Yup. So she shook her head like a dog at the beach, gritting her teeth and almost growling as she tried to find that anger again. Ah, there it was, she thought as she spat out another strand of hay and glared up at him, doing her best to stay focused on his disconcertingly mismatched eyes on his regular head and not the single-eye on that other head between his thick, muscular thighs . . .

"Perhaps we started off on the wrong foot," Adam said slowly, his hands still held out to the side in some gesture of peace, perhaps. A gesture that made his cock even more prominent. Why was he so hard? And thick? And long? And why were his balls so big? And . . . and . . . stop it!

"Your foot is not the issue here," she said firmly, her buttocks tightening as she held her steady gaze.

"Is it my eyes that trouble you?" he said, that half-smile showing again. "I was born like this. One green eye, one gold."

Ash shut her eyes tight and wondered if he'd be gone when she opened them up again. Gone, or at least clothed. Nope. Still here. Still naked. Still erect like this was an amateur porno flick. Why was he naked? Why was *she* naked? What was with the hay?

The memories came rushing back along with the thoughts, and Ash almost passed out again as the image of Adam Drake transforming into some kind of mythical beast appeared in her mind. The image was vivid, in full color, clearer than any photograph, more detailed than any memory. She blinked as she looked into his eyes, and she absentmindedly nodded when she realized it was the same set of piercing, burning, ultra-focused eyes she'd seen on the beast. One green. One gold.

"Your eyes don't trouble me," she said, the words coming out slowly, almost unconsciously as that image of his transformation burned bright in her mind. Then the image was gone, replaced by a sudden rush of emotion, energy pure and bright, primal and raw. It was energy that emanated from her core, her foundation, her essence. It felt like something was breaking through—or trying to break through. What was happening to her? Had he done something to her? Given her a drug or something? Was she hallucinating? Was she dying? Was she . . .

"You're a Shifter," she gasped, not sure why the thought had suddenly occurred just now while she was clearly dying of some awful dragon-transmitted disease. "Ohmygod, you're a Shifter!"

That half-smile disappeared from Adam's handsome face, and he cocked his head as he looked down at her. It appeared that he was confused for a moment, and then Ash saw his lips move like he was saying something, talking to someone else, perhaps to some*thing*else. She couldn't hear him at first because the blood was roaring in her ears like a waterfall in the mountains, but then his voice came through, clear and confident, with an undertone of barely-contained . . . joy?

"Yes, I'm a Shifter," he said softly as she gagged and choked, that primal energy inside her rising like an unstoppable force. "And so are you. So are you, Asheline Brown. You're a Shifter too, and the Change is coming. It's coming, Ash."

9

But all that came out of her was an animalistic scream, and then Ash was hunched over and gasping for air, holding her throat like she was choking, her brown eyes wide and bloodshot.

She is fighting the Change, said the dragon. *Just like you fought it for so many years.*

"I fought it because we would have burned the world and everything in it if I'd let you take control and do what you wanted," Adam snapped as he went down on his knees and held Ash by her upper arms. "Ash!" he said urgently. "It's all right. You're all right. Just breathe. Deep breaths, Ash. Look at me. *Look at me!*"

He spoke the last few words with authority, almost like an order, and as he heard himself speak, Adam was taken back to those years when he was Delta Force, given command of an elite crew of Special Forces men, put in charge. When he was Alpha.

A sudden yearning ripped through him, and he almost choked as his dragon roared inside him, bursting to break free once again. But Adam held it back, tightened the cosmic reins around his dragon and making it yield to him. It would not break free without his command again. He was in control. He was in charge. And right now he needed to be human for this woman. As human as he'd ever been. Perhaps more human that he ever thought he could be.

"My eyes," he said, lowering his voice as he went down on his knees directly in front of her. "Focus right here, Ash. You're all right. It's not time for you yet. It's all right. You can control it." He swallowed hard as he saw her brown eyes narrow to slits, and then suddenly it was her animal staring back at him, pure primal energy, raw and unrefined, all beast, just like his dragon.

A beast that wanted to get out.

A beast that wanted to break free.

A beast that wanted to run wild.

A beast that needed to be tamed.

"Control what?" she gasped, blinking and gasping again. Adam saw her animal withdraw, but then it was back in her eyes again, struggling to break free, to break out, to simply . . . break!

"Your animal. The other side of yourself. The side that is waking up."

"I'm not waking up! I'm freakin' *dying*!" she growled, and Adam heard the animal in her voice. It was strong. It was close to taking over, and if it did, things could get messy. Ugly. Violent.

Because if her animal took over when she wasn't able to control it, then Adam would have to take charge. And even though Adam was stronger, quicker, and more powerful than most men he'd met, he was no match for a Shifted beast while he was still in human form. If she Changed, he'd also have to Change to take control. And there was no animal in existence that could stand up to a dragon unleashed. Yes, things could get out of control if they both Changed, which meant he had to keep her in human form until she was ready. But how? She was losing it, he could tell. She had no idea what was happening, no clue how to tame her inner animal. What in God's name should he—

Take her, whispered the dragon. *Make her yours. Claim her now, as a human.*

Adam felt a chill rip through him even as his heat rose, his body stiffened, his grip on her tightened. By God, he wanted to take her! He could feel it in every cell, in every muscle, in every breath and thought. It had been years since he'd even touched a woman. It wasn't a lack of desire—it was fear of his own strength, his own power, of what he might do if he gave in to those primal needs. What woman would be able to handle the raw power of the dragon, even in human form?

This woman is yours, whispered his dragon. *She did not burn, and she will not break. She is your mate. She is your destiny. Your duty. Your obligation. Now claim her, or I will.*

The dragonblood was pounding in Adam's ears, his vision turning blood red like a curtain of crimson had been dropped down in front of him. He could feel the dragon inside him, but it wasn't trying to take over this time. It knew that this was a job for the human side. This was time for the man to take control, with the power of the beast in the background.

Claim her, the dragon whispered again, coiling itself within Adam.*Before she Changes. Make her yours so you can help her tame her animal. Claim your mate, you dumb human! Claim her!*

Adam looked into her eyes, brown and bloodshot, the inner battle raging inside as her pretty round face twisted in fear and anguish, her full red lips trembled with whatever was going on inside her. He'd made a mistake by telling her to let her animal come forth. It was too soon, and now he had to keep her in human form, bring out the woman in her, give a safe outlet to the power of the animal.

And so he grabbed her by the back of the neck, his cock rising to full-mast as he pulled her in towards him, the heat of their naked bodies sending up a wisp of magical smoke in the cold air. He pulled her in, pushed her hair back from her face, and kissed her. He kissed her hard, full on the mouth, like a man kisses a woman, like a man kisses *his* woman.

He kissed her.

By the talons of the eternal dragon, he kissed her.

10

She felt his fire as their lips touched, and then she was all fire, burning up inside, her heat rising so fast she swooned against his hard body, moaning out loud as she felt the beast inside her roar with approval. Her eyes were clamped shut, and it took a moment before she realized she was kissing him back, their tongues intertwined like snakes, their bodies crushed against one another, his massive cock pressed tight against her mound.

"Oh, shit, what's happening?" she gasped, breaking from the kiss for a moment before Adam tightened his grip on the back of her neck and pulled her back into him. He was so damned strong she was almost terrified, but the fear passed as ecstasy took over. She didn't need to ask any more questions. Her body was answering every question, and she had no choice but to give in, to dig in.

She dug her nails into his back as she felt his strong hands grab her buttocks firmly, his fingers spreading her asscheeks so wide her eyes flicked open in shock. She felt his blood on her fingertips as she dug in like a bear holding on to a tree-trunk, and she groaned out loud as she felt Adam's finger slide into her as he lifted her clean off the ground in the empty barn, rising from his knees with such power that she felt they might take off into the skies.

She instinctively raised her legs and wrapped them around him as Adam's cock lined up with her slit from beneath, and he held her there as he kissed her again. She could feel the massive bulb of his cockhead teasing her pubic curls, sending shivers of ecstasy through her as she tried to lower herself onto him.

"I am in control," he whispered, his eyes locking in on hers. She was mesmerized by his steady gaze, the sight of his green-and-gold eyes making her feel like she was locked in, locked down, at his mercy. "Of both you and your animal. Give yourself to me, and I will show you how to control that side of you. Give yourself to me, Ash."

She was breathing so heavy it sounded like an animal panting, and she whimpered as she felt him slowly lower her down onto his cock, rubbing his oozing tip back and forth against her stiff little clit as her wetness poured down on him like a river. She couldn't say a word, couldn't answer his question, didn't *need* to answer his question. She was his, she knew in that moment. She and her animal. His, and his alone.

Adam lowered her onto his cock as her thoughts melted into the heat of the moment, and as he filled her she felt her beast roar in submission, her animal accepting its Alpha, her woman accepting her man, all the way deep, all the goddamn way.

11

Adam could feel her heat envelop him as he lowered her onto his rock-hard cock. Her nails felt like claws on his back, and he roared as she drew fresh blood, her strong thighs tightening around his hips as he started to bounce her on his cock in a slow, hard rhythm.

"You are so hot inside," he groaned as he flexed inside her, his hands firmly beneath her luscious buttocks, his thumb pressed tight on her rear pucker. "And so goddamn wet. You are dripping all over my balls."

"What's happening?" she moaned, leaning her head back as Adam raised her up and then lowered her onto him, driving upwards with his hips and pushing so deep into her she screamed. "What's—"

But she couldn't even complete the question again, because Adam carried her swiftly across the barn, slamming her against the wooden walls as he pumped up into her, his dragon clenching inside him as he took his mate. He could feel himself slowly opening up the full range of his passion, as if he was instinctively seeing how much of him she could take.

"All of me," he groaned as he felt his balls tighten in preparation for what felt like an orgasm that was ten years in the making. "You will take all of me. Now and forever."

She screamed as he drove his hips forward and upward, driving and flexing his beast of a cock inside her, his shaft pressing against the inner walls of her vagina, the swollen head of his mast reaching deeper and deeper into her. Her fingernails were so deep into the flesh on his back that Adam knew it would leave marks even after healing. It would leave their mark on him. Her mark on him. Just like he was going to mark her . . . mark her from the inside.

He leaned his head back and shouted as his balls seized up and began to deliver his load, and as his cock flexed inside her and poured his heat into her valley, he saw images of the two of them running together, flying together, living together. He smiled as he came, the intensity of his orgasm rising like a spiral as she tore at his back, her heels digging into his buttocks, her wails and howls driving him wild as he pumped with all the fury of his manhood, all the power of his dragon.

And then his vision went blank and it was all fire suddenly, the image coming so quickly Adam gasped in shock, his fingers grasping Ash's hair and holding tight as he wondered what was happening. He blinked in confusion and stared into her eyes, and when he saw they were shining bright gold, iridescent like dragonfire but instilled with the wildness of the forest, he understood. He understood it all even though it made no sense.

He'd claimed her. He owned her. She was his.

She was his mate. She was in his arms. In his clutches. And she was coming.

By the wings of the eternal dragon, she was coming. Coming in hot. Coming in hard. Coming for him.

12

Ash felt his seed blast into her like hot lava from an erupting volcano, and she screamed and thrashed in his grip, tearing at his muscular back with her nails as he roared and pumped harder into her, every thrust of his pushing his massive pole of a cock deeper, seeking out depths she didn't know she had. His girth had stretched the lips of her vagina all the way, and her mouth just hung open as she felt her inner walls getting pushed outward as this beast of a man pounded into her, holding her tight against the wooden walls of the barn.

She swore the entire building was shaking as he took her with everything he had, and for a moment she didn't think she'd be able to take it, to take him, to take all of him. But then he came, his heavy balls slapping one last time against her naked underside until he went tight with the ecstasy of his release, his semen exploding deep inside her with such power that she swore she could taste him in her throat.

Ash's climax came screeching in along with his, and it took her a moment to even understand what was happening. Her vision had narrowed down to a singular point, bright red, glowing like the sun itself but somehow brighter, hotter, more powerful. She could feel him put something in her as he emptied himself with those frenzied thrusts, and as he filled her with his seed, that image of the sun was replaced by scenes of the two of them, scenes that hadn't happened yet: flying through clouds, racing through the woods, laughing together beneath mountain waterfalls . . . and then scenes of fear, panic, pain, Ash screaming his name as fire took over, death rained down, dread and misery ripping through her, coloring her orgasm with a dark undertone that somehow heightened the ecstasy.

"What's happening to me?!" she howled as she felt her wetness pour out of her, her climax spiraling upwards and taking her along with it. "What are you doing to me?"

He didn't answer, and she was lost again as her rising ecstasy hit its crescendo like a tidal wave crashing against the rocks, the climax splintering into a million secondary orgasms that shimmied through every part of her body. Ash screamed again, biting down without realizing she was doing it, her teeth sinking into Adam's shoulder as her nails clung tight to his back. She could feel his blood in her mouth, his semen in her vagina, his strength somehow flowing through her own veins, meeting some part of her that was waking up.

Finally, came a thought from inside her, a thought that was so crisp and clear she wondered if she was going crazy. Yes, she was going crazy. Or perhaps she was dead already. Frozen and stiff, hallucinating as she lost her grip on life. Yup. That was the only explanation that made sense. Everything else was nonsense. Being fucked by a dragon-shifter in an abandoned barn? Hearing voices from inside you as his semen dripped down your thighs? Yeah, she was dead and gone already. Might as well roll with it.

You are not dead, you dumb cow. You are just being born! Just waking up, came that inner voice that felt like her own but not exactly, like it was something more than what she was—or what she thought she was. *Just waking up to your true self. Good morning, Ash. Good morning, and welcome to the rest of your life.*

13

"Is it morning?" she asked as her eyes flicked open, the sight of the barn roof greeting her. She felt alert and alive, an energy rippling through her, warming her even though the barn had no heat and it was still winter outside, as far as she knew.

She felt movement beside her, and when she turned her head she was staring into his eyes, one green and one gold, both of them full of warmth and fire, ownership and possession, understanding and . . . love?

Ash jerked herself upright as the memories came roaring in: Bosco's Coffee and Cake; Adam turning into a dragon; the two of them making love like beasts in the Garden of Eden—or some twisted version of it! What. The. Hell!

"Is it morning? That's your first question?" he said, grinning as he glanced down at her naked breasts and then into her eyes. She didn't even consider covering herself—partly because there was nothing but scratchy hay around them, but mostly because he was naked too and for some reason it felt just fine. Natural. Normal. "You must be a very good journalist."

Ash frowned as she tried to fight back a smile. "I *am* a very good journalist, thank you very much. But . . . I mean . . . I think . . ."

"I know," he said softly, brushing a strand of hair from her forehead. "I don't understand it all either. But I understand more of it than you do. And together we'll figure out the rest."

"Together?" she said, her frown cutting deeper as she remembered what she'd felt when he'd taken her against the wooden walls the previous day.

"Yes, together," he said matter-of-factly, like it was a given, an obvious truth. He raised an eyebrow as he looked down at his shoulder, where she could see the faint outline of teeth marks. Her teeth marks.

She reached out and touched the faint marks, her frown so deep she was certain she was cutting new wrinkles into her face. "How did this heal so fast?" she said, licking her lips as she thought back to how she'd sunk her teeth into him in the throes of ecstasy. She tried to ignore the memory of how his blood tasted to her, to that part of her that she sensed was animal, pure beast, nothing but primal instinct. Of course, that was all part of the hallucination, she reminded herself. Part of the process of going bat-shit crazy.

"Fast?" said Adam, matching her frown with his own. "It took almost three hours! And your nail-marks on my back are still raw! My wounds usually close up within minutes, and they never leave marks on my body. Never."

Ash blinked, recoiling from his touch as a chill ripped through her, the memory of how those gold-and-green wings had ripped through his muscled back, how those shining scales had popped up all over his body, those jaws, those talons . . . ohshit, ohshit, ohshit!

And then she was gagging as the panic exploded in her, and she kicked at him and began to crawl on her hands and knees, wondering why she didn't stand up and just run. But then she felt her knees raise up off the ground, and suddenly she was on her hands and feet, power rolling through her haunches, a power she didn't know she had.

A moment later she had bounded clear across the barn, getting to the far side so quickly she was shocked. Where had all that power come from? Why was she bounding across the barn like an animal instead of standing upright like a human woman? What the hell? What the hell *was* she?!

"I don't know yet," Adam said, standing up and slowly walking towards her. "I know you're a Shifter, but I don't know what you are yet. Not exactly. It is curious. I cannot wait for your first Change."

"You're a lunatic," Ash said, panting as she pressed her back against the barn wall, pulling her knees up to her chest and staring up at him. "A goddamn lunatic."

Adam rubbed his strong jawline as he sauntered closer to her, his long cock swinging as he made no effort to cover himself. "A lunatic is someone affected by the phases of the moon. I am pureblood dragon. The sun gives me power, not the moon. You, however . . ." he said, trailing off and then shaking his head. "No. I do not believe you are a wolf-shifter. I think you are bear. Yes, that's it. A bear-shifter." He paused, a shadow passing across his handsome, deeply tanned face. "Interesting. Bears and dragons. A beast of the forest and a beast of the skies. Our kind have not gotten along in the past. But perhaps that is why . . . shit, perhaps that is why . . ." Then he grunted and blinked, focusing on her again like he'd chosen not to follow through on his line of thought.

Ash blinked as all those words swirled in her already-swirling mind: Bears, Dragons, Shifters. She shouldn't have understood anything he said, but somehow she did. Yes, she'd read about Shifters—

there'd been rumors for decades—but who would have believed they actually existed! As for his claim that she was Shifter and didn't know it . . . well, that was just . . .

"Bullshit," she said, hugging her knees and shaking her head violently. "Yeah, I saw what I saw at Bosco's yesterday. You turned into . . . something. I can't deny that, and I can't unsee that. And yes, I've read about Shifters, so maybe you are one. But me? No way. I'd freakin' *know* if I was a werewolf or something!"

"I already said I do not think you are wolf. Bear is my guess," Adam said nonchalantly. He furrowed his brow, his gaze moving over her body in a way that gave her tingles. He glanced down at her thighs and ass, which Ash was sure looked enormous because of how she was sitting. Then he grunted and nodded. "Yes, definitely bear," he said with certainty.

"Bear?! Did you just call me *fat*?" she shouted, glaring at him as the blood rushed to her face. She tried to suck in her cheeks, but she felt too puffed up with indignation to hold the look. "Why can't I be a sleek fox or an awesome tigress?"

Adam chuckled. "It is not a choice. You are what you are. Accept your animal, and you will be granted its power, granted control." Then he lost the smile. "But gaining control over your animal is not easy. Most Shifters fail, and when their animal takes over, it isn't good for anyone." He blinked and looked away, his eyes narrowing and losing focus for a moment.

"What? Are you talking about yourself?" she asked, wiggling her toes as she wondered why she wasn't freezing her big naked butt off. She looked down at her smooth skin, her neat little toes, her freshly waxed thighs. No fur or bear-claws yet, she thought with a strange mix of relief and . . . disappointment?!

Adam smiled, that faraway look still in his eyes. "The Change at Bosco's notwithstanding, I am in control of my dragon. It took years. Decades, truth be told. Most of that time I did not even understand what I was, could not comprehend what I felt inside, could not accept the part of me yearning to be given life."

"So then how did it happen for you?" Ash said, still looking at her bare arms and wondering if she meant *bear* arms. She giggled at the pun, deciding in that moment that she was either dreaming, dead, or simply insane—which meant she could do or say anything and it really didn't matter. As it was, she'd just "mated" a dragon-shifter in the middle of Wisconsin. Could this dream get any stranger? "And what's with this strange way of talking? You were in high-school with us. You were born and raised in the freakin' Midwest, weren't you? Why do you insist on speaking in that old-time accent? It sounds like you're in a Community Center production of *Pride and Prejudice*!"

Adam frowned, color rushing to his face along with a frown that suggested that perhaps it hadn't occurred to him that he spoke funny. "I was not born in Wisconsin. Or even in America. I do not remember my birth."

Ash blinked, not sure if he was serious. "Well, no one remembers their birth, really. But we figure it out somehow. There's like . . . records. Parents. Shit like that. And anyway, if you don't know where you were born, how do you know it *wasn't* in Wisconsin."

Adam ignored her. "This is how I have always talked. This is how people talked when I learned English. I suppose it stuck with me. As for my birthplace and parents? I do not care. What difference does it make?"

A chill trickled down Ash's bare (not bear) back as she studied his face. She really couldn't tell how old he was, and when she thought back to high-school, she realized that perhaps he did seem a bit old for the class. Also, she didn't have any memories of Adam from Middle School or anything before that. He'd sorta just appeared around Junior year in high-school. And then he was gone before the end of Senior year. Less than two years. There and gone like a wisp of smoke, almost like he was just doing a fly-by.

"How . . . how old are you?" she asked, cocking her head and blinking as that chill stuck with her just like his words. "Please don't tell me you're like a thousand years old, because I am gonna freak out. Seriously. Do *not* tell that you've been flapping around in the skies while . . . while, shit I don't even *know* what was going on in the world a thousand years ago!"

Adam just shrugged, folding his arms across his chest. "Much of the same. Wars. Oppression. Conquest. Chaos. Violence. Just with different weapons. Also, there were no iPhones."

Ash snorted like a little piglet, hugging herself and rocking back and forth as she decided that yes, she was dreaming. No way was there a thousand-year-old naked man standing in front of her, talking like he was an aristocrat from the 1300s, telling her that she was actually a bear-shifter . . .

"So . . . so how could I be a Shifter? Was I Turned at some point?" she said after a moment. "Like when a vampire bites someone and they turn into a vampire?"

Adam leaned his head back and laughed. "Hah! There is no such thing as a vampire! How ridiculous!" He laughed again as Ash stared in disbelief at this man—who'd not so long ago turned into a golden-green dragon—now giggle at the notion that vampires might exist. All right. Whatever. This was a dream anyway, right?

"Why were my clothes burned off?" she asked.

"You were freezing to death as I carried you in the skies. My dragon bathed you in blue flame as we flew, and you did not burn. The dragon believes it is because you are my fated mate. Legend has it that a dragon's true mate is immune to his dragonfire. The only thing in the world that can survive his heat. But I do not think . . ." Adam took a breath as his words trailed off, and Ash blinked and looked down at the ground. She could feel that something had changed inside her. Something was different, a mix of something old and something new.

"Fated mates? Fate? As in destiny? Meant to be?"

Adam shrugged. "My dragon is a sentimentalist."

Ash laughed. "So your dragon believes we're fated mates and you don't?" she said softly, heat rising through her body as she said the words. Then she looked up at him, directly into those burning eyes. "What do you believe?"

Adam held her gaze without blinking. "My dragon and I are one. Two sides of a coin. And although the dragon is raw instinct, unbridled power, primal energy, it is also my connection to ancient wisdom that exists in the cosmos."

"So that's a yes then?" Ash said, half-smiling as she tried to figure out if this guy was for real. Of course, none of this was real, so she might as well have fun with it. "Where's my wedding ring? Or is that not a thing for Shifters? You just kidnap me, pound me against the wall of some old barn, and then step back and say it's fate? How romantic."

Adam grunted, a half-smile breaking on his darkly handsome face. Then another grunt, but no more words. He began to pace, rubbing his stubbled jawline, his muscular buttocks shining in the splintered sunbeams that were breaking through the old barn's tattered roof. Finally he turned, those eyes narrowed again.

"Romance is not a part of it. If we are fated—and it remains to be seen if the legend is true—then we must simply accept it," he said with almost no emotion in his voice.

Ash raised an eyebrow. "Um . . . so it's like an arranged marriage?"

"Marriage is for humans. We are Shifters. More than human. Above such silly, meaningless traditions."

"Excuse me? *More* than human? How arrogant can you get? We're humans first, thank you very much! At least I am. You seem more like a piece of stone than anything right now," Ash said, frowning even as it occurred to her that this was the most ridiculous argument she'd ever had. What the hell was she hoping to accomplish by even engaging in this fight? Why did it even matter what this beast thought about marriage or romance or any of it! Was she actually buying into his fated mates bullshit? Was she buying into *any* of it?! Shifters?! Humans turning into animals at the full moon or whatever?! What was this, some cheesy paranormal romance novel?!

"We are more than human, and when your first Change occurs you will understand it," Adam said, his voice still devoid of emotion, almost like he'd flipped a switch. "Though you already know it deep down. You know you are a Shifter, just like I knew even as I denied the truth for years as a child and young adult."

Ash closed her eyes and shook her head firmly. "I don't know anything. And how could I be a Shifter? My parents were . . . normal," she said, swallowing hard as she paused at the word normal. It almost seemed insulting to suggest that Shifters weren't normal. But whatever. Political correctness could wait. Right now she had some other shit to sort out. Like maybe find some clothes?

"I will bring you some clothes shortly," Adam said without hesitation or explanation, and it seemed like he'd read her mind. Or perhaps she'd spoken out loud. Or maybe just looked down at her naked boobs, making it clear that she wasn't *all* animal yet. There was still good 'ol human shame, the need to cover your fat ass in public. "First I want you to think back. Was there an event in your past that you remember?"

Ash pouted and stared sulkily at him, not sure why she was pissed off. "An event? Like a birthday party? Graduation? The last episode of *Lost*? Yeah, I remember lots of events, genius."

Adam took a long breath, and when he exhaled she smelled smoke in the air. A chill ran through her when she realized that she was angering him, pissing him off, that perhaps he wasn't kidding when he said that a dragon was all about rage, all about fury, all about fire.

"I mean an event with a bear," he growled, swallowing hard like he was trying to hold back his dragon. She felt the fear make her heart beat faster, but there was also a strange defiance in her, a mix of perverse confidence as she locked eyes with her "fated mate" or whatever he was. Hey, he said she was immune to his fire, right? So let him huff and puff all he wanted.

"I did get a nice teddy bear for my fifth birthday," she said, doubling down on that feeling of perversity, wondering how much she could annoy him before he exploded. "And my friend Polly and I do have a bear-claw feeding event most Sundays. Any other questions?"

She saw his fists clench, and for a flash she swore those dragon-scales popped up along his naked bronzed body before disappearing as he tightened his jaw and stretched his neck.

"If you do not want my help, you are free to leave," he said through clenched teeth. "But trust me, that bear inside you wants to get out. And there is no telling if the dragonfire has affected you as well, affected how quickly the Change will occur. And although I am quite certain you are bear, there is no telling what kind of beast will emerge from within you."

"Emerge from within me? Sounds like the plot from the movie*Alien*," Ash muttered, shaking her head and sighing. "All right, fine. Since I don't really want to hitch a ride on Highway 95 in my birthday suit, I'll bite. An event, you said? Like being attacked by a bear? Something like that?"

"Exactly like that," said Adam, calmness returning to his body. "Blood contact."

Ash thought for a moment, but there was nothing like that in her past. She was sure of it. She'd remember being attacked by a goddamn *bear*!

"No," she said firmly. "Nothing like that."

Adam took a long, slow breath, frowning as he glanced at her. "Then you are a natural born bear. Which means that one or both of your parents are Shifters."

"No," said Ash, blinking as images of her parents came rushing back. Fleeting, faint images. It had been decades since they'd been flown back to Milwaukee in sealed caskets on a military jet, the coffins wrapped in the American flag. "They died when I was seven. But I certainly don't remember them turning into freakin' *bears* at the full-moon or whatever."

"The moon has nothing to do with it," Adam said. "A Shifter who has gained control of her animal can Change at will. It is likely they did not Shift in your presence. Perhaps they wanted you to have a normal childhood. Perhaps there was some other reason they held back." He thought a moment. "Any siblings? Brothers or sisters?"

Ash blinked as she stared at him. Only now as she

answered his questions did some of the patterns begin to fit together. She still had no idea what the patterns meant, but there was something here, something in her past, too many unexplained gaps to be simple coincidence. "I had an older brother. He was much older. I barely knew him. He joined the military when I was kid. Missing in action. Presumed killed in combat. They never found his body."

Adam jerked on his feet like he'd been hit in the face, and his eyes widened as he stared into her eyes. "An older brother? A bear Shifter in the military? Are you—"

"I told you, there was no *Shifting* going on! As for Bart, I don't even remember what he looked like, I was so young! What are you—"

"Quiet. Just let me think. This cannot be. It is too much of a coincidence." He studied her face like he was searching for something. "Who are you?" he whispered, and she could see the paranoia in his eyes, hear the suspicion in his voice. "Who sent you? Where did you hear my name? Was it Benson? Someone else in CIA Black Ops? Tell me the truth and I will let you live."

"What the hell are you talking about?" Ash said, her head beginning to spin as the madness of the past twenty-four hours began to catch up with her. Suddenly she felt light-headed, dizzy, faint. She hadn't eaten or drunk a thing in a day. And now this naked dragon-man was whispering nonsense about fate, destiny, alien bears exploding from her body, and some paranoid tin-foil-hat level ramblings! Or something like that.

"A Shifter immune to dragonfire," Adam said, clenching his jaw, his eyes going wide. "The only creature that can kill me."

"What?" said Ash, blinking in confusion. "What the hell are you . . . wait, do you think I've been sent by the government to *kill* you? You think I'm an *assassin*?!" She snorted, her brown eyes going wide as she stared at this madman. Yup, Adam Drake was still a nutcase. And she was naked and alone with him. Great. Just freakin' *great*!

She wanted to say something more, but Adam was acting weird and she just cocked her head and stared.

"What are you doing?" she asked with an almost amused frown.

But Adam was ignoring her, his lips moving as he muttered something under his breath. She couldn't make out the word. It sounded like nothing she'd ever heard. Maybe a name? The name of his dragon?

"Ohmygod, are you trying to Change?" she said, taking a step back as the thought of those wings exploding from his back struck a chord of fear in her, wiping away all traces of amusement from her face. Maybe she was immune to dragonfire, but what about dragonclaw? Dragontooth? Dragontail? That beast could still rip her wide open or squash her like a freakin' grape!

But there were no wings and no talons and no lizard-tail the size of a semi-truck. Instead Adam just paced in anger, muttering away like he was fighting with his dragon, like he couldn't command the Change, like his dragon was straight-up refusing to come out!

She watched as Adam raved and ranted, fists clenching as he paced, every muscle in his beautiful naked body tensed and flexed. For a moment she almost felt sorry for him. She could see that he'd been affected by a life of loneliness, decades of roaming the Earth as a one-of-a-kind freak, living with a power that had to be a curse as much as it was a blessing. Who knew what he'd been through in the military, what had happened on that secret mission he'd mentioned. Had he been living his entire life thinking that he was on some government hit-list, that he'd be eliminated the moment they figured out exactly *how* to kill an ancient, fire-breathing monster?

"Adam," she whispered, the chill of fear transforming into a strange warmth . . . the warmth of feeling, the comfort of understanding . . . and below it all the simmering heat of . . . of love?! No, of course not. She didn't even know him, and what she did know should make her run for the hills! But she couldn't fight the feeling, and as she watched this tall, troubled man fight his own feelings, his own demons, his own doubts, she was suddenly sure of it.

Fate.

Fated mates.

That was why his dragon, that carrier of ancient wisdom, was refusing to come forth. It knew. Somehow, it knew, just like something inside her knew. Her essence. Her core. Her intuition. Her . . . animal?

She felt something move inside her, a power coursing through her veins as she gasped and staggered, almost overwhelmed by what she felt. What was happening to her? Was this real? Was any of this real?

She felt her animal inside her, and she watched Adam struggle with his own beast, the two of them naked and bare, exposed to one another while fighting with what lay within each of them.

"It's not going to work," she suddenly said, the words coming from a place she didn't know existed, the confidence in her voice surprising her. "Your dragon isn't going to respond. This is about the human in you. The man in you. Our animals already know what we are. It's just the humans in us that need to come to terms with it."

Adam stopped pacing, his angry mutterings trailing off as he looked towards her. He held the gaze for a long time, so long it seemed like time itself had slowed down, perhaps even stopped.

"How can I believe anything you say?" he whispered, his eyes burning with a doubt that Ash could tell was coming only from the human in him. "You show up out of the blue, saying you just want to catch up. Then it turns out you're a Shifter who's immune to dragonfire. And now you're telling me you're Bart's little sister?! I should kill you just for being related to that asshole!"

"Wait, what? *What*?!" Ash said. "You . . . you knew my brother?"

Her head spun as the coincidence hit her like a smack to the ass. What was happening here? Maybe there *was* a conspiracy going on—a conspiracy that even *she* didn't know about! Was she being played too? Played by someone in the government? This John Benson guy? Were they trying to flush out Adam and they were using her as bait? Maybe they'd been watching her for years, wondering if she was a Shifter just like her brother? Maybe they'd figured she was the only one who could flush out the dragon, get him out in the open? Who knew what was coincidence and what was conspiracy! What was fact and what was . . . fate?

Control yourself, you dumb cow, she thought as she took deep, heaving breaths. You're an investigative journalist, right? So freakin'*investigate*! Ask questions! Just talk, you moron!

Adam was about to say something else, but she cut him off with a crisp, concise question, her tone gentle and smooth, like she was talking to a riled up pet. Instantly she saw Adam calm down, and she could feel her own animal relax too, as if in agreement that this was the right course of action, the right path.

"Tell me about him," she said in that soft tone, knowing she just needed to talk, just needed to get Adam to talk. "About my brother. About you and my brother. Tell me, Adam. Please. Just talk to me. It's all we can do right now. It's the only way we can figure out what's going on."

14

Adam was barely listening. He'd tried to Change, but the dragon hadn't responded. The dumb beast was just sitting there in the background, clearly disobeying his order! What the hell was happening to him?! First the dragon takes over without being called—at a goddamn coffee-shop, that too! And now the dragon *refuses* to come forth?! When had that *ever* happened?! *Why* would that ever happen?!

When unleashed I could kill everyone in the world, whispered his dragon finally, *but not our mate. She is immune to dragonfire. There is no clearer proof that she is ours, and yet you talk of conspiracies and assassins like some fool? I am ashamed of my human. I would be embarrassed to even show up at the annual dragonfest—if there were an annual dragonfest. My dragon-friends would laugh at me—if I had any dragon-friends, of course. If I had any friends at all.*

Adam almost laughed as he listened to his dragon sound as close to a love-sick puppy as it possibly could. This beastly part of him that could literally reduce the world to ashes giving him advice on . . . love?

Ashes, he thought as he paced furiously, running his hand through his thick black hair, rubbing his unruly stubble. Ashes. Ash. Fate. Coincidence. Conspiracy. What was the truth? What should he do?

Adam stopped and turned to face Ash. He just looked at her. Into her eyes, brown and big, wide and innocent, but with a curiosity that burned like his fire, a depth that reached into his soul, energy that activated his dragon and his human. He'd tried to forget everything about where he'd come from, but it was clear she wanted to know where she came from. All right, he thought. You aren't going to kill a naked woman, bear-shifter-assassin or not. So maybe you just start talking and see where it goes.

So Adam took a long breath as he looked into her eyes, and then he blinked and just started talking.

"Your brother was Special Forces too—Army Ranger," he said softly, his body tightening as the memories came back. Memories that started with the joy of being in a crew—being the *leader* of a crew. The focus that came with working with other powerful

Shifters, bringing them together to accomplish something meaningful, channel their animalistic energy into doing some good instead of running wild. And then it all went to shit. Fuckin' bears! Uncontrollable beasts! What was he doing with another of them?!

"I already knew he was Special Forces. But that's a start," Ash said. She waited and then raised an eyebrow. "Um, you can keep talking now."

Adam blinked when he realized he'd gone quiet, the memories taking over. Shit, he'd been alone so long he'd forgotten how to have a real goddamn conversation! Thinking and talking were basically the same to him. Inside voice and speaking voice sounded the same. Damn, he was far gone!

He took a breath and nodded. "We were put together with a few other Shifters that had made their way through the military. For some reason the military attracts Shifters—even ones that don't know what they are yet. Anyway, we were a secret group that almost no one knew about even at the highest levels of the government. The blackest of Black Ops. Full Dark." He grinned, but not because anything was funny. It was almost a grimace. "We lasted one operation. A holy mess of an operation. That's why I know what happens when Shifters don't have control of their animals."

"Different animals . . ." Ash said slowly, and Adam could see the wheels turning, her sharp mind taking notes. She was smart, he could tell. A smart bear? That was a change. "So my brother the bear. You and your dragon. Who else? Or *what* else, I suppose."

"There was Caleb," Adam said. "Wolf shifter. A lone wolf. Very powerful. And a couple more in the background—big cats, a silverback gorilla, maybe others. But we never saw them. The grand Shifter Project blew up on the first try. Our entire crew had to split up, disappear, melt into the darkness, each one of us getting as far away from the other as possible. The combined power of a group of different Shifters, different animals, different beasts, was too raw to control, to wild to manage, to primal to be put on a leash."

You were supposed to be the leash, you fool, whispered his dragon, interrupting Adam's thoughts. *And you still are that leash. You are destined to control that power. You were born to be the alpha. You were just not ready then. An Alpha cannot be in control of a crew without finding his mate first. Now your mate is here. Your fated mate, the one who will bring balance to us, balance to the crew. She will bring a steadiness that will allow you to control the crew, to accomplish great things as they each find their fated mates, gain full control of their animals, balance the human and the beast, the light and the darkness.*

"Stop talking like a thousand-year-old mystic, you overgrown lizard," Adam muttered through his teeth. "Let me handle this. Yes, it's a strange coincidence that she is Bart's little sister. But—"

"Who the hell are you talking to?" Ash asked, her eyebrows rising as she stared at him like he was insane. Which, of course, he might be, Adam thought. After all, he *was* talking to an invisible overgrown lizard that breathed fire and whispered advice directly into his brain.

"Nobody," Adam said quickly, blinking and looking away.

"Wait, are you talking to your . . . your *dragon*?" she said, her eyes going wide. She leaned forward, squinting as she looked deep into his eyes. Then she waved and smiled. "Hello! I'm Ash! What's your name?"

Adam felt his dragon surge inside him, its natural state of rage fueled by the simplest of questions that was in fact the most profound of questions for a Shifter. *What's your name.* Had she seriously just asked his dragon its name?! Was she trying to control his animal?! Did she even know what she was doing?

"No!" he said sternly, tightening his body as he felt his back ripple, those mighty wings aching to burst free. Then he looked into Ash's brown eyes, her pretty round face, her full lips. She was a delightful mixture of childlike innocence and the strength of a woman in her prime, and Adam felt a strange fullness in the center of his chest as his lips opened up into a smile. "No," he said again, softly this time. "You don't ask the name of a Shifter's animal. That is the most guarded secret, something that is between human and animal, a secret that is shared only when the human masters himself, takes control of his animal. Knowing your animal's name will give you power to Change at will, at your command. It is hard-won knowledge. It takes years to get there, decades sometimes, perhaps even a lifetime. You cannot just trivially *ask*! That is simply not going to—"

"Godzilla?" Ash asked, blinking innocently as she teased him. "Lizard-face? Or perhaps you went to the other extreme so no one would guess its name! How about Fluffy? Peanut? *Muffin*?"

Adam felt the heat roar through his veins as his dragon thrashed within him, yearning to break free, to spew fire at the insult, to punish this woman for her insolence. Punish her in the most delightful way. He almost let his dragon take over, but he knew it could mean disaster. All that sage advice notwithstanding, what lived within him was all beast, all rage, all fire. Yes, Adam could call it forth at his command, but once he Changed and the dragon was unleashed, things could always go either way. Fated mate or not, the dragon was perfectly capable of swallowing this sassy reporter whole, hair and toes included, end of story. She could find her happily ever after in Fluffy's reptilian belly!

"What are you doing?" he asked, swallowing hard when he saw the strange perverseness in her brown eyes. She'd started off just teasing him, but there was an edge in her voice by the end of it. Almost like she was taunting him, challenging him!

It is her animal trying to break loose, growled his dragon. *Let it come and we will show her who is in charge. Bring on the bear.*

Adam ignored his dragon and kept his focus on Ash. Her breathing had quickened, her breaths coming short and fast, like little snorts. Her eyes had narrowed, the brown in them turning bright to where they were almost gold. Her fists were coiled like claws, and now slowly she stood, her bare feet firmly planted in the rough ground of the barn.

Do I let this happen, he wondered as he watched the Change start to come over her. He'd stopped it earlier, keeping her in human form by taking her as his mate. It had felt like the right thing to do then, but for some reason Adam held back now. It had taken him years to control his own Changes, but this woman might be different. Perhaps she would be able to handle her Change. Perhaps she—

"Tell me your name," he heard her whisper as she arched her neck upwards. Her eyes were glowing, pure gold like fire, and Adam felt his dragon coil inside him at the sight. Gold was like a drug to his dragon, and Adam let out a low hiss as he watched Ash talk to her animal, asking its name like it was nothing.

"Careful," he muttered as he held back his own Change. It took an effort that surprised him, and for a moment he lost focus on Ash just so he could manage to control his own animal!

And in that moment of lost focus it happened. With

an ungodly sound that started as a scream and ended as a roar which shook the walls of the barn, Ash
spread her arms out wide, her naked body turning
bright gold, her hands turning into big brown paws,
claws curved like scimitars emerging from what used
to be fingers.

She'd swiped across his chest before he knew what
was happening, and Adam shouted when he felt his
skin rip, smelled his own blood in the air, felt the
drops roll down his body. And then he was dragon,
his wings bursting from his back as he rose up in the
air and prepared to hold down her bear, to get control
of her animal before it did something that couldn't
be taken back.

But when he looked down from twenty feet up in
the air, Ash was gone. In the few seconds that it took
for Adam to Change, she'd smashed through the walls
of the barn and headed out into the snow, roaring as
she raged across the land.

"Oh, shit," Adam shouted as he blasted his own
path through the poor barn, which now looked like
it had been bombed and shelled. "How the hell is she
so fast?"

Adam took to the air and gazed down, his laser-focused sight immediately picking up on the beautiful
golden beast tearing through the snow. Her feet were
barely touching the ground, and it looked like she was
gliding across the land.

"Oh, my God, you're beautiful," he whispered as he spread his wings and glided above her, watching as her beast tasted freedom for the first time, felt what it was like to simply run, to simply *be*! He remembered the first time he'd flown as a dragon, and although it had been a different set of circumstances, that joy of freedom was the same. He knew how she felt right now, and he knew he had to let the Change run its course. All he could do was watch over her, protect her from herself, make sure her bear didn't do anything that would get the National Guard after them!

But just as the thought came, Adam heard the sound of distant thunder. He turned his massive scaled head upwards, but there wasn't a cloud in the sky. It was clear blue, the sun beating down on the pristine, snow-covered land. He must be hearing things, he decided at first, turning his attention back to the joyful sight of his mate experiencing her animal for the first time, like a pup playing in the snow!

Then he heard it again, and he realized he knew that sound. He'd know it anywhere. It was the throaty, full-bodied rumble of jet engines, the roar of jets flying close to the speed of sound. Impossible, he thought as he spun in the air, instantly taking in a full view of the horizon. A moment later he picked out the three dots in the distance. Three dots that were getting larger. Three dots that were unmistakable to Adam.

Three fully-armed fighter jets coming in hard, coming in hot, coming for them.

There could be no mistake. After all, he'd flown the damned things before discovering he had his own wings, his own fire! But these metal dragons had serious firepower too, he knew. And although his scaled body could handle the heat of a goddamn nuclear explosion, his mate was exposed, out of her mind, oblivious to what was going on, what was about to happen.

And then for the first time in perhaps his entire existence, Adam Drake felt fear. Fear that he might lose something that mattered. Fear that he might lose something that belonged to him, that was precious to him, that was *his*!

In that moment every drop of dragonblood in him heated to the boil. Dragons were possessive by nature, hoarders of wealth and material goods. But this sort of possessiveness was different from what Adam had ever felt. The possessiveness over a mate. The need to hold on to his mate, his woman, this beautiful creature bounding across the land. The need to protect. Protect with his life. Protect with death, if need be.

And as his dragon took over, that otherworldly rage bursting to the forefront, Adam felt his world changing as the fire burst from his open throat like a missile of pure anger, a vehicle of absolute destruction, a gush of unbridled madness. Everything was red the next moment. Everything was fire. Everything was death.

And when he saw those planes explode in the air, when he realized what he'd done, what he'd let his dragon do, what he'd let *himself* do, everything went dark.

Dark forever.

15

"**T**here is no going back," Adam said, his tone without emotion, without life, dark and dead. "Not from this. Not after what I did."

"You did it in self-defense," Ash said, but her own voice was soft and unsteady. Her memories were hazy at best, but she could feel the crushing guilt that racked Adam's body. She could hear it in his voice, see it in his eyes—eyes that seemed darker, almost dead.

"No," he said, looking straight ahead, looking through her, his eyes unfocused as the rolling sand dunes stared back at him. She wasn't sure where they were, but clearly this wasn't Wisconsin. This was desert. They were somewhere in a desert, and it didn't feel like America. Africa? The Middle East? Once

more she closed her eyes and tried to remember, and
slowly the images came back, almost like they were
responding to her command.

"Oh, God," she murmured as the feeling of being
her animal in the flesh came rushing back, the sensation of pure instinct washing over her like a wave
of unadulterated joy. It was pure freedom, pure nature, nothing but energy in its most basic form. She
smiled as she remembered how it felt to have four
paws digging into the snow, powerful haunches driving her along with breathtaking speed, the knowledge
that she was strong and beautiful and . . . and *herself*!

In her memories she could see the shadow above
her, the dark shadow of the dragon, Adam Drake, her
mate. He was gliding above her as she glided over the
ground. He was watching over her. Protecting her.
Loving her. She knew it then and she knew it now,
and she blinked away a tear as she looked up at this
stoic military man, this loner dragon, this man who
she instinctively knew was nothing but good and
honorable but was now broken by what he'd done . .
. what'd he'd done for *her*!

"Oh, shit, it wasn't self-defense!" she blurted out.
"Bullets and missiles wouldn't do a thing to your
dragon! You did it to protect me! You did it for me!"

"I did it because I lost control, gave in to the dragon's rage, the madness of the beast. I was weak," he
said, still not looking at her. "You made me . . ."

He trailed off, and a chill went through Ash as

she finished his sentence in her head. *You made me weak.* She understood what he meant, and the thought filled her with a sickness that made her shiver even though the desert sun was blazing down on the two of them. She closed her eyes again, no longer wanting to think about what Adam was going through. She wanted to ease his pain, but she wasn't sure how. She barely knew him, even though she felt connected to him in a way she couldn't understand.

Perhaps he just needs to be alone for a while, she thought as she sighed and kept her eyes shut tight. The memories were still coming, and her lips trembled when she saw Adam's dragon spin effortlessly in the air to face the oncoming jets, its green-and-gold wings blazing bright in the winter sun. The dragon roared as it faced the triple threat, spreading its wings like a shield over its mate down below. Then the beast arched its massive head back, opened its gigantic maws, and spewed fire like an avenging demon.

Ash winced as she watched the fighter jets burst into flames, and she sobbed as she saw metal and debris rain down on the earth. There could be no doubt that the pilots had been burned alive like . . . like . . . whoa, wait! What was that?! Go back, memory! Go back a minute!

Her memory responded with a clarity and quickness that astounded Ash, and she blinked as she replayed the scene with the dragon turning in the air to face the incoming jets. Yes, there it was. It could be her imagination, just wishful thinking, but in her memory she could see the canopies of each jet pop off and the pilots ejecting clear just as the dragon unleashed its wrath onto them. It was strange, the way all three pilots ejected at almost the same time, like they were responding to an order.

"Adam," she said, her voice trembling with excitement. "Adam, you didn't kill those pilots! They ejected just before your dragon destroyed their planes. All three of them. I see it as clear as day!"

"How can you see it when you were looking? You were running wild, your bear in control, your paws on the ground, your face in the snow," Adam said sullenly.

"I don't know how, but I see it, Adam. Clear like a video in my freakin' head. All three pilots blew their hatches just as you were turning to face them. I saw their parachutes open up just as you swooped down to lift me up. They're safe, Adam. I'm sure of it! You aren't a killer!"

Adam snorted, shaking his head and looking at her with pity in his eyes. "You know nothing about me, Ash. I am *all* killer! What do you think I do when I Change? Plant daisies in neat rows in my flower patch? No, Ash. I kill. I burn. I destroy. That is the essence of the dragon. It is a part of me, and that's why I live here, in the desert, where death is all around,

where evil abounds and I can channel my killer instincts into perhaps doing something useful for the
world."

Ash blinked and looked down, not able to hold his
burning gaze. He was right. She knew nothing about
him. In fact, what she thought she knew about Adam
Drake might be all wrong, which meant she actually
knew *less* than nothing about this lone dragon!

"You're right," she said softly, rubbing her bare
arms and wrapping the sheer white satin robe around
her body. She wasn't sure where Adam had gotten
the robe from, but she was somewhat glad she wasn't
still naked. Adam, however, was bare as the day he
was born. He seemed comfortable in his own skin—
human or dragon—and Ash felt her heart speed up
when she remembered that she was animal too, she
was Shifter as well, she was . . . oh, God, what *was*-
she?! Was she a killer as well? A monster like Adam
said he was? Was this her fate, to roam the Earth like
an outcast, a one-of-a-kind beast who was no longer
human, would never be accepted as a human, would
never be "normal" again?

You were never normal, she reminded herself, biting her lip as she told herself she wasn't going to cry.
Bears don't cry. Monsters don't sob. Beasts don't
bawl. You always knew you were different, that your
family was different. You sensed it, and now you
know. So instead of freaking out, why don't you learn

about it, learn about yourself, learn about who you are, what you are, *why* you are! Wasn't that the story? The most important story? This whole thing had started off as a chance to get a story, and what was bigger than this, than your own story?!

But it's more than just my story, Ash thought as she looked at Adam, stoic and naked, his dark mood seemingly unchanged by the news that he hadn't burned those pilots, that they'd made it out alive. In that moment she knew Adam had taken lives before, that his darkness was real, his guilt was deep and unshakeable, the conflict so raw it was laid bare on his smooth, bronzed face, cut into the chiseled muscles of his body. It's his story too. It's *our* story.

She blinked away the hint of a tear, swallowed the rising anxiety about herself, and forced herself to focus on the story before she went insane. Whether she was a werebear or a goddamn bandicoot, whether Adam was a killing machine or a flying machine, she still had a career to think about, right? Right. So here goes. Ask questions. Ease the tension. Do what you do! Just freakin' *talk*!

"So what do you do here, alone in the desert?" she said.

"Sorry, what?" Adam said, jerking his head toward her. Clearly he'd been lost in his own thoughts. "What do I *do*? You mean for money? Or like hobbies or something?"

"Yes, sure. Let's start with money. Are you just rich? Or do you not need much money out here?"

Adam snorted, his eyes lighting up at the mention of money. "I don't need a lot, except for new clothes. I tend to rip through my own." He chuckled as she smiled, and Ash could feel the mood immediately lighten. Had anyone asked Adam anything about his life? Had he even had a real conversation in the recent past? "Yeah, I don't need a lot of money if I think about it. My dragon, however." He grunted and shook his head. "You don't know much about dragons, do you?"

"No. Does anybody? So enlighten me."

Adam sighed and looked up at her. She could tell that the dark cloud was lifting from over him, and it made her heart feel light and bouncy. She pulled her robe around her and nodded for him to go on.

"Dragons are . . . hoarders. Collectors. Possessive to the extreme," he said in a low voice. "Gold, jewels, land . . . any form of wealth is like a drug to a dragon. Anything that can be owned, *must* be owned."

He was looking at her with those gold-and-green eyes, his gaze steady and unrelenting. Then he smiled and looked past her, as if he'd chosen not to say anything more about what else he felt was his, what else his dragon had claimed, possessed, taken as its own.

"All right," she said, swallowing as she felt the energy between them, a connection that felt so real she could almost reach out and touch it. Just keep talking, she told herself. Focus on the story, or else you'll lose your shit with all this craziness. "OK, so you do make money. How?"

"I'm a bounty hunter."

Ash cocked her head. "A bounty hunter? As in you hunt bad guys for money? Like in the Wild West?"

Adam shrugged. "Sort of. It's now the Wild East, though. But yes, I hunt bad guys for money. Gotta pay the rent."

Ash glanced around them. There was no structure in sight. It was just the two of them sitting on a freakin' sand dune in the goddamn desert. Whatever. She didn't want to go to his underground lair just yet. So ask a different question. "So these bad guys . . . who are they?" she asked.

Adam shrugged again. "Known terrorists. Insurgents. War lords. Genocidal maniacs. You name it, I kill it. And Uncle Sam pays me once I send in proof that the job's done."

"So you work for the U.S. government," Ash said, feeling the excitement of the story starting to rise in her blood. "You're still Special Forces. Or Black Ops. Secret missions sort of thing."

Adam snorted and shook his head. "I work for no one. I told you, that great Shifter experiment with the U.S. government ended after one mission."

"But the government pays you, which means you work for them," Ash said.

"May I finish?" Adam said, frowning and shaking

his head, letting a thin smile show on his handsome face. "You know, a journalist should let the person she's interviewing say a few words too."

"Thanks for telling me how to do my job," Ash snapped, frowning even though she was holding back a smile. "Now are you going to answer my question or should I just answer it for you?"

"Go ahead, Miss Hot-shot Reporter. Let's see what you got."

Ash took a breath and narrowed her eyes. "Well, I do know that the U.S. government keeps a running list of known terrorists and other unsavory characters, each with a bounty on his or her head. Usually this means that they pay for information leading to a capture, but . . ."

She trailed off as she thought back to what she knew of the world of political bounties. Yes, the official story was that the bounty was for information. But it was a not-so-well-kept secret that the government would still pay the bounty if it was a kill done by private military contractors. She knew for a fact that there were rag-tag groups of ex-military men all over the Middle East chasing down bounties. The money was good, depending on how big a fish you caught. Yup, she thought as she remembered seeing bounties as high as a million dollars for some high-value targets. The money was *very* good.

"Ok, so you're a private military contractor," she said, thinking out loud as she connected the dots that made up the picture of Adam Drake. "And you must be very good, or else I wouldn't have heard your name from one of my sources."

"You heard my name? What sources?" Adam said sharply, leaning forward, his naked cock swinging as he came close.

Ash glanced down at his manhood and then hurriedly back into his eyes. He really was an animal, the way he seemed completely without shame when it came to his body. Again she felt herself wondering if she was going crazy, if this was all a dream. Stop, she told herself. Get a grip. She glanced at his cock again, feeling the color rush to her face. A grip on yourself, not on . . . *that*!

She blinked and forced her gaze upwards. "Um, can we continue this conversation without . . . I mean with . . . I mean . . . you know what I mean. Clothes. Cloth. Body coverings. Please."

"Is my natural form distracting?" Adam said, grinning as he straightened up and placed his hands on his deeply tanned, muscular hips. "See, this is why I like the desert. No rules. No laws. No—"

"This is about basic decency, not laws or rules," Ash said. "Would you stand like that if this were a video interview?"

"No," said Adam, changing his pose to one where he tilted his hips up in a comically vulgar position. "I would stand like this, so the high-definition camera can capture the full extent of my glorious—"

"Eww," Ash yelped, shielding her eyes and giggling at the atrociously beautiful sight of his massive cock and balls thrust forward in the most shameless manner. It should have been disgusting, but it felt so open and natural that she couldn't help but laugh. They *were* animals, it occurred to her. And animals feel no shame about their bodies. Anxiety and self-consciousness about your body was a purely human thing.

For a moment she was taken back to those glorious moments when her bear had come forth, when human and animal were one, gliding effortlessly through the snow, the sun shining down on her golden fur, her dark claws glistening like they'd been freshly chiseled by the gods themselves. It still seemed like a dream, totally unreal, like it had happened but of course couldn't *possibly* have happened! She couldn't *possibly* be a . . . a . . .

Focus, she told herself as she stared at Adam. Don't lose it, girl. If you really are a Shifter, then you've got a lot to learn from this man. This beautiful, bronzed, muscular, naked man with . . . OK, *focus*! And *not* on his goddamn crotch!

"You know I can't tell you about my sources," she

said, forcing herself to focus on his face, those green-and-gold eyes. She swore she could see the dragon in him, the beast looking directly at her, looking *into* her perhaps. It sent a shiver down her back, but it was the shiver of excitement, not fear. She wasn't scared of his beast. Her bear wasn't scared of his dragon.

My *bear*? Why are you even thinking like that? Where are these thoughts coming from? Have you lost your mind, girl?

"All right then," Adam said, breaking her out of her thoughts before she lost herself in them. "So what did you hear about me? Why did you contact me out of the blue? Under false pretext, I might add."

"What false pretext?" Ash said.

"Your email. You said you wanted to meet for a date, not an interview to advance your career."

"It was *not* a date!" Ash said, her eyebrows going wide as the color rushed to her face again. "It was not a date," she said again with a firmness that took some effort.

"It was clearly a date," Adam said equally firmly. "And a successful one at that."

"Successful? How do you figure?"

"Well," said Adam, and Ash couldn't help notice his cock move. "We met at a coffee shop, and then I took you home with me. Textbook definition of a successful date."

Ash snorted in disbelief. "Um, you turned into a

monster, destroyed the building, carried me off in your freakin' talons, and then proceeded to have your way with me in an abandoned barn. Not sure what textbooks you've been reading."

"Better than reading Shifter Romance novels," Adam said with disdain. "Cheesy crap that totally misrepresents our kind."

"Oh, so you've read a couple, have you? Good. We're moving on to your hobbies now. I guess it must get lonely out here in the desert."

Adam grunted, eyeing her up and down, his cock filling out in the most obscene way as his gaze rested on her heavy bosom, her big red nipples hardening in response beneath the sheer white cloth. "A dragon does not feel lonely. If anything, it is getting a bit crowded out here now."

"Well, perhaps I should leave," Ash said, glancing down at his rising erection and then shrugging. "I'm sure you can handle yourself from here on."

He grinned, his gold eye flashing as if the dragon inside him was stirring. "You're going to leave before getting your story? Tsk. Tsk. Disappointing."

Ash smiled. "Ah, so you're going to give me my story? Answer my questions?"

Adam took a breath, his eyes twinkling. "I'll answer three more questions."

Ash thought for a moment. "All right. I'll play. Question One: How old are you?"

"Old enough. Next question."

"OK, you're supposed to actually answer the question. That's the rule."

"I make the rules. Next question, please. You have two left."

Ash felt the competitiveness in her rise, but she took a breath and nodded. "All right. Question Two: Were your parents Shifters? Dragons?"

"I never knew my parents," Adam replied, the words coming so quickly Ash was certain they were a lie. Or at the very least there was something more to that answer, something he wasn't telling her, something he perhaps was denying to himself too. She made a mental note and moved on without pushing further. Her reporter instincts told her to hold back on this one for now. This scaly beast, despite his comfort in hanging out completely naked, was not going to open up to her just yet.

"All right," she said, sighing and rolling her eyes. "Third question. You said you—"

"No more questions," Adam snapped, his eyes narrowing and shining bright as he shook his head.

"You said three!" Ash protested, putting her hands on her hips and glaring up at him.

"Well, I changed my mind."

"Oh, you changed your mind? How convenient. So basically your word is worth shit. Your promises are meaningless."

Adam grunted. "Better you learn that now, little girl."

Ash almost doubled over in shock at his sudden change. "Little girl? How dare you call me that! I'm a grown woman, and I've—"

She stopped herself when she realized he was just taunting her and she was playing into his hands by rising up and taking the bait. She didn't need to justify herself to him! She didn't give a shit what he called her! "Overgrown lizard in the body of an ape," she muttered under her breath, her chest heaving as she tried to control her anger. She'd never been particularly hot-tempered, but she could feel the rage bubbling inside her, a wildness that almost scared her. Was that her bear? Was she a bear? A freakin' *bear*?!

"What did you just call me?" he said, frowning and clenching his fists.

But Ash wasn't in the mood for games anymore. She didn't give a shit about what he was or wasn't anymore. She was annoyed, pissed off. To hell with this rude asshole. Who cared what he was. The only question that mattered now was what *she* was! It all seemed like a dream, perhaps a nightmare, hopefully an hallucination. But she could feel the animal inside her, and that wasn't her goddamn imagination. She wanted to get up and leave, go back to her old life. But how? What would she do back in Wisconsin? She was a bear! She needed . . . help! Shit, she needed help!

"Help me," she said, all that focus lost in an instant. She didn't want to ask him for help. But she had no choice. She was alone in the goddamn desert, with an animal inside her, a freakin' bear that was clawing at her insides like it was trying to get out again. Suddenly all that bullshit about mates and fates and whatnot didn't matter. She was panicking. Straight up *freaking out*! "Help me understand, Adam. What am I? What do I do?"

Adam took a breath, his hands still on his hips as he looked down at her from his towering height. She could see the conflict on his face, like he was somehow torn between helping her and simply turning his back and walking away. She couldn't understand it, and it only made her confused. Then it made her angry, made her bear angry, made *all* of her angry!

"You want to know what you are, then go find your brother and interview that out-of-control asshole," he said through gritted teeth. "He ruined it for all of us. There was a chance for the Shifters to find a place in this world, to harness their animals to do some good. But your bone-headed brother lost control of his bear and screwed it up. I don't want anything to do with bears anymore. I am sorry I brought you here. I will take you to the nearest U.S. Military Base and drop you off. You are on your own from there. And so am I. If there's anything I can teach you about Shifters, it's that we're meant to be alone. Doomed to be alone."

16

Adam felt his dragon hiss and roil as he said the words. He couldn't believe what he was saying. This was his mate. He'd taken her, claimed her, poured his seed into her. Hell, she was immune to his dragonfire, something he didn't even know was possible! She might even be pregnant with his offspring! His babies! *His*! And now he was turning her away?! What was he doing? Was he insane?

He looked down along her curves, his body tightening as his dragon whispered for him to take her again, to claim her once more, to make her his and keep her with him. Images of Ash big and pregnant flashed through his mind, and Adam clenched his teeth as he fought them. He knew it was the human in him that was fighting that need, fighting his dragon, fighting his very nature. But he also knew he could not give in. His dragon was powerful, with access to ancient wisdom that existed in the cosmos. But the dragon was also just dumb instinct, raw power that cared nothing for logic or common sense. Life as a Shifter was all about control, all about the strength of the human to stay in charge. Yes, it was about strength, and taking a mate made you vulnerable and weak. Ash was proof of it, wasn't she?

Hell, in just a day he'd lost control of his dragon twice around her! First he'd Changed in a goddamn coffee shop in Milwaukee! Then he'd blasted three American fighter jets out of the sky in a display of overprotective behavior for his mate! Yes, the pilots had somehow ejected before they'd gotten turned to toast, but that was besides the point. His dragon didn't know and didn't care whether the pilots were safe or not! His dragon was out of control around this woman! She had to go! Now!

"What?" she said, blinking as the color left her face. "You want me to . . . to go? You bring me here? Do this to me? And then send me away? What kind of a man are you?"

"Not the kind you want to be around," Adam said, looking away past her towards the distant horizon. The sun was slowly setting over the desert skies, and soon it would be night. "This is for your own good. It is also for the good of the world. Dragons and bears are not compatible. Nothing but destruction can come of it. You saw what happened with those fighter planes. It took all of three seconds for my dragon to burn them to the ground."

"Yes, I saw that. And I'm still puzzled by what those planes were doing there. The American military isn't allowed to engage within U.S. borders."

Adam grunted. "The rules don't apply when a hundred people report a flying monster above downtown Milwaukee."

"Yes, the rules apply. The rules always apply! I don't think those planes were going to fire on you. I think they were there to escort you out of civilian airspace. That explains why those pilots all ejected at almost the same time, just when it was clear that your dragon was going to attack."

Adam froze, his jaw clenching tight as he stared at Ash. She was smart, and perhaps she was right. If those planes were there to attack, they'd have fired at him from a long ways away. He'd flown planes himself. He knew the range of their missiles. The only reason they'd come so close would have been to try to control him, to do exactly what Ash had said: Escort him to where he wasn't a danger to civilians. As for the simultaneous ejecting by the three pilots . . . shit, that would only have happened if they'd been given an order by someone watching.

He glanced up into the sky, frowning as he scanned the darkening blue canvas dotted by the emerging stars. His dragonsight narrowed, and soon he picked up the telltale flashes of satellites and drones high above the earth. The government had eyes in the skies everywhere, and no doubt someone had been watching Adam and Ash. Someone who instantly knew when the dragon was out of control, when it was time to give the order to the pilots to get the hell out of there.

"Benson," Adam muttered, blinking as he thought back to the man who'd created the Shifter task force, the man who'd given the Shifters a chance, the man who'd believed these animals could be harnessed for good and not just destruction. The man who'd been proven wrong by Bart, Adam, and the ruthless wolf shifter Caleb. "John Benson."

"Who's John Benson?" Ash said, and Adam almost kicked himself for saying the name. He'd been alone so long that he was used to thinking out loud. Yet another reason why this wasn't going to work. He wasn't cut out for a mate. Certainly not one with an inquisitive mind and connections to the world's press! What was he thinking, bringing her here!

Adam's mind swirled as he considered his next move. He couldn't keep her here, that much he'd decided. She made his human weak, made his dragon wild, and was a disaster waiting to happen. The incident with the fighter planes had proved he didn't know himself around her, that he was a danger when that protective instinct kicked in, that dragon-instinct to hoard, to hold on to what was his, to dig in and never let go. Imagine how bad it would get if she actually had babies! His dragon would burn any living creature that came within a hundred miles of his brood! And then John Benson would not be giving an order to escort him or control him. The next order would be to put him down like the out-of-control beast he was!

No. There was too much at stake. This was about more than just him. There were other Shifters out there, and Adam had to keep his unspoken promise to stay out of sight, to let his dragon do its damage in the lawless deserts of the Middle East. That was the price he'd paid for that screwed-up operation. That was the price they all paid. Bart the Bear. Caleb the Wolf. Who knew if they were even alive?! Who knew, and who cared! Dumb furballs! Never trust an animal with fur! They'd had their chance and they'd blown it!

But she still deserves a chance, does she not, whispered his dragon, which had been quiet all this while. *She is innocent of your mistakes, the mistakes of your Shifter crew. Besides, she is your mate, and we know it. Take her, Adam. Keep her. Hold her. Love her!*

"Shut up, you dumb reptile. She isn't staying,"

Adam muttered, turning away from her as he tried to keep his voice low.

Fine. Send her away. Send her away and see how the universe brings her back to you, takes you back to her. You cannot fight fate, just like you cannot deny who you are. The sooner you accept it the better for everyone.

"Who's everyone?" Adam whispered. "Clearly not the poor humans who get in the way when you run wild with your lizard-brained protective instincts."

This is about something bigger. Dragons are loners, but they still have the primal need to mate, to reproduce, to protect and cherish their young. Dragons are also leaders, and bears and wolves need a leader. They need an Alpha, whispered the dragon. *They need you.*

"You're crazy," Adam grunted, shaking his head. "The last thing I want is to babysit a bunch of out-of-control furballs."

You will not have much of a choice in a few months, the dragon replied. *The fur-balls are coming. Cute and tiny. Roly-poly, with cherubic round faces and green-and-gold eyes.*

Adam frowned as he turned back to Ash, his gaze moving along her mesmerizing curves before coming to rest on her round belly. He could feel it already. His seed was in her, and it had taken. Like it or not, she was going to pop out some furballs—or whatever the hell kind of little monsters would result from their union. He could also feel the truth of everything else his dragon had said. He'd felt that obligation to be the Alpha even when it was just Bart, Caleb, and him in the crew.

He'd felt that obligation, and he'd turned his back on it.

He'd turned his back on his duty, his brothers, his crew.

The realization slashed through him like a set of talons, and Adam almost roared out loud in anguish. He'd blamed Bart and Caleb for going off the rails, losing the plot, straying from the path. But it was him, wasn't it? Adam was the one who'd failed! Bart and Caleb were young, wild shifters who needed an Alpha's steadiness, leadership, guidance. The instincts to be part of a pack, a crew, a tribe ran as deep as the drive to mate, but Adam had rejected his calling, rejected *them*! Just like he was trying to reject this new calling, this deepest of callings, this woman with curves that made his dragon go wild! A Shifter whose animal had awakened, a Shifter who just might be proof that the legend of fated mates was real . . .

Destiny, whispered his dragon. *We cannot run from it, fly from it, or burn it down. So you might as well give it a chance. Give her a chance. You owe her that much.*

"I owe nobody anything," Adam muttered through gritted teeth. "That is how I have lived my life, without owing a thing. Debt is poison. Responsibility is a burden. I fly free, free of all attachments. You understand that better than anything, you dumb dinosaur."

I understand the call of destiny, the pull of nature, the dragon replied. *And you feel it just like I do. It is just your human brain that is overthinking it. If only you turned over the decision-making to your cock and balls it would be so clear we would not even be having this conversation.*

"What the hell is going on?" came Ash's voice, stopping Adam just before he replied. "Are you talking to your dragon again? What's it saying?"

Adam closed his eyes and let out a long, slow breath, wondering what she'd think if he told her what his dragon had just recommended. Balance, he told himself. Compromise. That has been the key to controlling your dragon, and that will be the key to controlling this situation. Meet the dragon halfway. Meet this woman halfway. Give her something, and then step back to your solitary life, where you can fly free above the burning sands once more, just like you were born to do. The dragon feels the pull of lust, not destiny. Do not give in. Give a little, and then stay on your path.

"It's saying that I should give you your story. Your *own* story," he said. "It's saying perhaps I owe you something after putting you in this position, awakening your animal, bringing you out into the desert, giving rise to so many questions about who you are, about *what* you are."

"Well, whoop-dee-doo," said Ash, clapping her

hands gently and snorting. "At least one of you has some sense of honor and responsibility. So what's the story? I can barely wait. I mean *bear-ly* wait. Hee hee!"

Adam groaned and shook his head, trying not to reward her with a smile. "I will help you find your brother," he said after a moment. "If he is still alive, perhaps it will help shed some light on who you are. I will help you find him, and then . . . well, then you are on your own."

He felt his dragon chuckle as he said the last few words, but there was still a part of Adam that was convinced that taking a mate was a bad idea. Dragon says yes. Human says no. Burning dragonheart says yes. Cold logic says don't be a goddamn fool. The conflict between his human and his dragon had never been clearer—not for decades—and it made him feel a restlessness that made his body tighten for a release.

But he pushed back against his dragon. Adam the man knew what he was doing. That incident in Wisconsin had blown this thing wide open. There were photographs of him all over the Internet. Maybe even videos of him Changing! This story was breaking, and it was stupid to think he could shut it down now. There'd been rumors of Shifters in the fringe publications for years, and now it was about to go mainstream. The only thing to do was to give this woman the story and then get the hell out of the way, step back into the shadows, return to the depths of the desert, where no one would ever see him again. The life of a dragon was lonely. That was the deal. That was his fate. Maybe she was pregnant from that moment of weakness when he couldn't control his need to mate. But probably not, right? Who knew if it was even possible for her to have his kids! Either way, that was her damned problem. He wasn't going to be Daddy Dragon. There was no such thing.

"And then I'm on my own? Suits me just fine. I've done just fine on my own," Ash said, her eyes narrowing, her round face hardening. "Let's see what you got. I think this is just a cop-out so you don't have to answer my questions about you, about where you came from, your past. My brother's been missing pretty much my entire life. If he were alive, I think he'd have sent me a goddamn postcard. This is just a wild goose chase to distract me from the real story, which is *you*. But whatever. I'll bite. Let's go."

Adam snorted. "A postcard from Bart the Bear? Right. That would be the day. I doubt that big lug can even hold a pen in his meaty paws."

"My brother is dead," Ash said firmly, crossing her arms beneath her breasts again, making Adam blink as he tried not to stare at the outline of her big, dark red nipples. God, he would love to suck on them right now, feel their hard points in his warm mouth, suck so hard she groaned and fell into his arms again as he took her.

But Adam turned from her to hide his swelling manhood, snorting again. "Maybe he's dead, yeah. But I don't think so. It isn't so easy to kill a Shifter. You saw what I did to those planes. And although Bart doesn't fly, he's got other . . . . qualities." Adam paused when he realized that Ash might share some of those ferocious bear-shifter traits that had made Bart a force of beastly nature on the battlefield. God, what if they had babies? How powerful, how beautiful, how amazing would that combination be?! Adam felt a sickening warmth in his heart as once again that image of Ash pregnant and full came rushing back to him like a photograph, like it was already true. And then that overwhelming need to possess her, to protect her, to claim her now and forever. No. No. *No*!

"So you really believe my brother is alive after all these years of hearing nothing—not from him, not from my sources, not in the news," she said slowly, blinking and staring up at him as if she was trying to figure out if this was all a trick. "If he's an out-of-control bear-Shifter, wouldn't someone have noticed? Taken a picture or something?"

Adam shook his head, a tight smile emerging. She wasn't ready for this. Wasn't ready for what it meant to have a Shifter lose control of his animal. "Not if he killed anyone who came close to taking a picture."

Ash's face turned the color of . . . well, ash. She stared at him as her breathing quickened, and Adam could see her connecting the dots, realizing that maybe her brother was in fact alive, understanding that finding him would give her not just the story of the Shifters, but the story of her own life, her own past. Perfect. Maybe then she wouldn't notice when he disappeared on her.

"What about my parents?" she said, her voice shaking. "Did you know—"

"No," said Adam, looking away from her. "I knew nothing of them. Bart didn't talk much. He mostly .. . broke things." He took a breath as he tried shake the image of Ash and him together, raising a bear-dragon family. No way that would make him happy. He needed to wipe those thoughts out of his mind, stick to his cold, logical decision to give Ash her story and then disappear. But shit, it was hard to get the image of her curves out of his mind. That pesky dragon and its monster-sized need to mate was taking over. Perhaps he needed to release some energy, wreak some havoc, dragon-style. Appease the beast, remind that overgrown lizard that sex and violence came from the same source, that they were much better at ending lives than creating new ones. He could feel his dragon stir as Adam thought about flying, burning, unleashing that dragon, and he smiled. "Anyway, these are questions for Bart, not me."

Ash blinked, her eyes taking in the sight of his naked body in a way that told Adam she was becoming

more comfortable with nakedness—a sign of the animal in her. "Why are you always deflecting questions
about yourself? What are you hiding? What are you
hiding from, out here in the desert?"

Adam grunted and narrowed his eyes toward the
setting sun, forcing himself to tear his gaze away
from her beckoning curves, her relentless questions,
questions that were awakening parts of his past he
didn't want to deal with—never wanted to deal with.
His restless dragon strained within him as a thin
smile tightened his lips, a dark idea came to his swirling mind. Yes. Why not. She wanted answers? She
wanted to see why he was out here in the wild desert
all alone? Then show her. Show her who you really
are, *what* you really are. Then watch her run for the
hills. Problem solved.

Yes, when she sees what it truly means to be with a
dragon, she will not want to have anything to do with
you, with us, Adam replied in his mind as he considered that next move. He reached for a rucksack and
pulled out his satellite phone, a wicked grin breaking
on his face as he scrolled through the latest list of the
CIA's Most Wanted, selecting an interesting renegade
Sheikh with a solid $750,000 bounty on his bearded
head. Dead or alive, just the way Adam's dragon liked
it. His smile was so wide his face hurt, and he chuckled softly as he felt his dragon rumble in approval,
like it was saying, "All right. Why not. Let me out, let
me burn, let me eat . . . and we're all good."

It felt good, but there was also a darkly perverse thrill from the human side of him. This move was serving his logical human brain's needs as well. Common sense told him he could not take a woman into his life—not long term. Especially not this woman, who in a day had proved that she would always be a source of vulnerability for him, a source of weakness, a source of straight-up trouble. If she saw him at his worst, understood that he was a beast who spewed fire and crunched on human bones like they were pretzel sticks, she'd understand that he was never going to be a nurturing, loving mate. The only romance he and his beast understood was the romance of swooping down from the clouds, reveling in the screams of horror as the dragon burned and fed.

"We are flying," he said again. "But we just need to make a quick stop on the way."

17

"**Y**ou know," Ash shouted as they flew through the twilight above the Syrian desert, "when someone says they need to make a quick stop on the way, they usually mean like at the grocery store for milk."

"I don't drink milk. My dragon is lactose intolerant. But we get enough calcium from bones."

"Bones? What does that mean?"

"You'll see," Adam replied.

Ash closed her eyes as the warm air blew her hair back. Then she remembered it wasn't hair. It was fur.

Her fur.

It all felt like a dream, and Ash shuddered as she thought back to earlier, when she'd stood there barefoot in the sand, gasping as Adam rose to full height, his naked bronze body shining in the setting sun. She'd gone dumb as she watched him mutter something that sounded like a command or code-word, perhaps a freakin' magic spell—who knew!

And then it had happened, his Change in all its glory. Gold and green shining wings bursting out of his back, iridescent scales glistening on his body, arms and legs turning to enormous haunches with shining black talons, head arching back to reveal gruesome teeth that were somehow pure white like ivory. It was a terrifying, horrifying, petrifying sight, and it should have made her want to bury her head in the sand and pray for it all to end, to go away, to just*stop*!

But she couldn't turn away from him, and she could feel her bear growling on the inside, pushing against her to break free. She frowned as she willed herself to hold it back, and she felt the animal roar as it retreated just enough to give her control. A strange satisfaction went through her when she realized that perhaps she*could* control her own animal, that maybe she wasn't going to randomly turn into a bear at the most inopportune moments, that maybe she could still live a normal life as a Shifter.

What the hell is normal now, though, she'd wondered as the dragon turned its massive scaled head towards her, its green-and-gold eyes focused on hers.

"Hop on," came the voice from the dragon. It had

the essence of Adam's voice, but it was deep, unreal, its dark timber resonating through her entire body. She didn't think she could refuse if she tried. The power of the dragon's presence was too overwhelming, too all-encompassing, too goddamn awesome.

"Um, OK," she said, blinking as she hitched up her long white robe and wondered how she was going to climb on this massive beast. "Do I step on your . . . um . . . feet? Pull myself up with your wings? How do I . . ."

"Change," commanded Adam. "This is not a pleasure trip. I cannot have a human woman screaming in my ear as I rain hellfire on these murderous bastards. Besides, you will not be able to hang on with your weak hands as we fly and twist in the air. Not to mention we might get into a firefight. You will need your bear's strength. You must Change."

"Um . . . OK . . . but how? I don't . . ."

"You will have to learn. Learn how to control your animal. And it all starts with learning how to control the Change. Because once your animal comes forth, it is in charge until you learn how to find a balance within yourself, to understand when to give the animal free rein and when to pull it in, make it kneel, make it submit to your will. That part will take years, perhaps decades. Do not expect to simply—"

"Done," said Ash brightly, looking down at her hands as they turned into massive paws almost instantaneously. She felt the energy of her animal roar through her, her blood heating up as her body expanded. She could feel her butt morphing into the muscular haunches of the beautiful brown bear that was her animal, and she leaned her head back and squealed in delight.

Of course, the sound that came from her was no high-pitched squeal but a throaty, full-bodied roar that she was sure would be heard for miles. She grinned and pawed at the dry sand, her eyes shining with glee as she tensed up her body and then leapt up onto the dragon's back, digging into its tough scales with her sharp claws.

The dragon roared as Ash dug in, and she just laughed and dug her claws in harder. "Stop whining, you big lizard! You asked for this. And I don't understand why you make such a big deal about controlling the Change. I said Change, and now I'm a bear! Did it seriously take you ten years to figure out how to do that?"

Adam had grunted as he turned his head up to the sky. "Changing to your animal is not the challenge. The tricky part is Changing back. An untrained animal will not want to give up control. Let us see how easy it is for you to go back when the time comes." He paused for a moment. "Still. Good job with the Change," he'd muttered, his voice revealing that he was perhaps just a teeny bit surprised—perhaps even impressed—with the control she seemed to have over her bear so early. "Now hang on, and try not to gouge out my eyes. I need them to fly."

Ash had roared in delight as they took off, the dragon's mighty legs pushing up off the sand as its massive wings caught the air currents and carried them up above the rolling sand dunes. She'd lost herself in the beauty of just being alive, and it was only when she saw the distant caravan of three Toyota Land Cruisers, each of them modified to have a machine-gun mounted in front of the sun-roof, that she realized this wasn't a joyride.

"Sheikh Ahmed," Adam rumbled as he circled high above the caravan. "Well, he's not really a Sheikh. No royal blood in him. He just took the title Sheikh after claiming control of a small part of the disputed territory between Syria and Iraq. He travels with a small raiding party, all of them brutal men with multiple kills behind them. Kills that include civilians. Women. Children. And American soldiers." He paused as he made a giant circle in the skies, and Ash could feel the dragon preparing to dive.

"Um, what are we . . ." Ash began to say as the realization dawned on her that this wasn't a seek-and-capture mission. This was . . . "Oh, God, you're going to kill him?"

"Correction. I am going to kill them all. Burn them brown, and then eat them," replied Adam. "Though we will need to hold on to Ahmed's head so we can collect the bounty."

"Hold on to his . . . *what*?!" Ash screamed, her voice getting drowned out as the dragon completed its turn and went into a deep dive, the air whistling past her ears as they descended at breathtaking speed. "Are you *crazy*?!"

"This is my life, Ash," Adam roared through the wind. "I am a bounty-hunter, a beast, a man with no name, a freak with no morals. This is who I am. The earlier you see it, the better for everyone."

"Can we talk about this first, please?!" Ash yelled, but she could feel her bear's jaws open wide in delight, her tongue hanging out. Her animal was loving this, and Ash hated herself for it. Suddenly she understood what Adam had told her earlier about what would happen when her animal was in control, how those primal, wild needs would take over. And what were the needs of a bear in the wild? Why were bears some of the most feared beasts of the forest?

"Talk all you want," came the dragon's voice. "But excuse me for not replying. I have some burning to do."

"Oh, shit," she muttered as the shouts of the terrified men came up to her flattened bear-ears. The cars had stopped, and men were scrambling to turn those sinister machine-guns up towards the unholy winged beast swooping in on them. A winged demon being ridden by a golden-brown bear, its jaws open wide in a hideous smile. "Oh, *shit*!"

The throaty roar of three machine-guns erupted in

the air, and Ash screamed as Adam raised his wings and shielded her from the bullets. She could hear the shells bouncing off his steely scales, and she gasped in shock when she realized she was safe, that he was protecting her, that he was in complete control of the situation.

She felt the heat of dragonfire rip through the body of the beast as she straddled him, and a moment later a blaze of white-hot flame blasted from Adam's open maws. The sensation was sublime, and Ash almost choked at the rush of exhilaration that went through her as she felt Adam's power between her legs. She was roaring as she held onto him, her claws firmly lodged between his scales, her animal howling in pleasure as the adrenaline flowed through woman and bear at once.

I'm a beast too, she realized as she watched one of the three cars explode in a ball of beautiful flame. Two of the insurgents were thrown clear, and they scrambled to their feet, not giving a damn that their robes were on fire as they ran for their lives from the horror descending on them. But the dragon circled round and dove, grabbing one of the men in its talons, his bones crunching to powder between the dragon's powerful claws.

Ash screamed in shock when she realized what was happening, that Adam and his dragon were killing people. Bad people, yes. Evil people, sure. But he was freakin' *killing* them!

"No!" she shouted even as her bear roared in approval, and she could feel the conflict within her, the conflict that Adam had warned her about. The conflict that she would need to resolve if she was ever going to be at peace with who she was: Part animal, part human. Half woman, half beast. "Adam, stop! We can't!"

But the dragon was in control, and Ash knew it. So she just stared as the dragon swooped down on the second man, opened its jaws wide, and swallowed him whole. Just like that he was gone. A slightly burnt appetizer. Insurgent flambé.

In a daze Ash looked down at the scene. The insurgents from the second vehicle had already abandoned ship and were running willy-nilly in all directions, some of them turning and firing the odd shot. The bullets whizzed by, and even the ones that hit just bounced off Adam's dragon-armor. Ash was quiet now, her vision ultra-focused, the adrenaline in her system narrowed down to a steady buzz that was like a drug she knew was going to be addictive. Her animal was alive and alert, in full control now, its dark brown eyes taking in every little movement, its big ears capturing the smallest of sounds.

As the dragon corralled the few runners and made short work of them, burning a couple, eating one or two, and then killing the last one with a lazy swipe of its massive tail, Ash heard a strange metallic sound, a large click that send a shiver through her, woke up her instincts.

"Adam!" she shouted when she turned her head

and saw that one of the insurgents had mounted a rocket-propelled-grenade launcher on his shoulder and was taking aim. "Adam, turn! Get that guy before he—"

But the dragon was breathing fire and dispatching death, completely oblivious to everything around it. Ash stared at the man with the RPG, and then, without even thinking, she crouched down on her powerful haunches and leapt off the dragon's back, her bear-claws spread wide, the roar of her animal the only sound she could hear.

18

Adam felt her weight leave his back just as he swooped down to crunch up the last of the fleeing insurgents from the first two cars and turn his attention to the last vehicle, the prize catch.

"Ash!" he roared, panic ripping through his dragon as he wondered if his mate had been hit by a bullet. There would be no holding back the dragon's mad rampage if Ash was wounded or worse, and the realization terrified Adam as the fear of losing her mounted. In that moment he knew he would burn the world and everyone in it if something happened to Ash, to his mate, and that was a sign of the ultimate weakness, the ultimate loss of control, the ultimate defeat.

He twisted in the air, his long neck turning as he

prepared to dive and catch her before she hit the ground. But then he saw her beautiful brown bear, its long golden hair flying in the wind, its paws spread wide, claws out, jaws open. Ash hadn't been hit. Ash was doing the damned hitting! Her bear was in control, all that primal instinct to hunt prey and rip flesh awakened as she sensed a threat to her territory, her mate, her . . . family?

"By the talons of the eternal dragon," Adam muttered as he pulled back in flight and watched his mate land square on the man with the grenade-launcher, her claws driving into his chest and ripping it wide open almost effortlessly. "She is . . . she is . . . she is *beautiful*! Yes, she's goddamn beautiful, and she's mine. All mine."

The man was dead before his eyes got to close, and Ash's bear just flung his tattered body off the roof of the car. A moment later she'd ripped through the metal roof itself, pulling out another screaming man and tossing him over her shoulder like a ragdoll.

Adam's dragon roared in delight, swooping in and catching the man in mid-air, ripping him apart and swallowing half of him, letting the rest fall to the blood-stained sand of the desert. Then there was just the prize left, the illegitimate Sheikh with the bounty on his head. The dragon was in ecstasy at the wild carnage being unleashed, but its instinct to hoard was also in effect, that need to build wealth, the ancient dragon-instinct to stockpile gold and jewels and whatever else was a sign of riches.

"We need his head," Adam whispered as he flew close to his bear-mate while she cornered the evil Sheikh. "Save his head."

A chill went through Adam as he turned in the air once more, his neck twisting just in time to see Ash tear out the Sheikh's throat with her bear's jaws. This was no ordinary bear Shifter he realized. *She is Bart's sister, part of that same bloodline. Without control she is vicious. I cannot unleash her on the world! I cannot just walk away from her now. Her animal needs to be brought under her control. Only then might I have the luxury of walking away and returning to my life of solitude.*

Sounds good to me. Good compromise. Or good excuse to stay with her, whispered his dragon. *Not that you need an excuse, but whatever helps you sleep at night, whatever makes sense to your tiny human brain. All I know is that she is your mate now and she will always be your mate. There is no returning to that lonely life. Now that you have found her, everything will change. Shifters around the world are slowly waking up, those dormant genes are being activated. Pandora's box is opening up, and there is no walking away. The dragon is destined to lead, and this bear from an ancient bloodline will walk by your side. There is a war coming, and you need a warrior like her by your side. There is no other way. No oth-*

er option. Too little too late. No escaping your fate. No running from your mate.

"There you go with the bad poetry again," grunted Adam as he circled above the scene and gazed down at his warrior-mate, her bear standing up on hind legs, its blood-stained snout open wide as she roared to the heavens, roared to the gods, roared to her mate. "Nice try, but this has all the makings of a great tragedy, not a romance. Look at her. She's a wild beast!"

So tame her, whispered the dragon. *Tame the she-beast that is your mate. Tame her, Adam.*

19

Ash screamed as she tasted the blood, felt the energy of her animal take over so completely that she worried she'd lost the human inside. What had she just done?! How was she capable of this?! She hadn't even thought about it before she leapt off the dragon's back and ripped a man wide open down the seams! How could she ever control her animal?! How could she ever trust herself not to turn into a beast the moment someone crossed her?!

She howled mournfully up at the darkening sky, her mind swirling as she stood up on her bear's hind legs and circled round and round. There was fire and death all around, the taste of blood and the scent of burning flesh. She was in hell, wasn't she. Yes, she was in hell.

"Oh, God, I want to die!" she sobbed as she saw what she'd done. "I'm a monster! A murderer! A killer! A . . . a . . ."

You're an animal, came a whisper from inside her, and somehow she knew it was her bear. *And that's what animals do. It is the way of nature. The way of the wild.*

"Well, I don't *want* to be wild!" Ash shouted, and as she heard herself she understood that the human woman was very much alive inside her. It gave her hope. Just a glimmer of it, but still hope. Hope that she could somehow control this power. Channel it into the right outlets. Use it for good. Wasn't that what her goal was as a journalist? She could've made more money doing celebrity gossip, but she'd chosen investigative reporting instead, worked her way up to the point where she was taken seriously.

We do not get to choose who we are, answered her bear. *We are what we are. Accept it. Embrace it. Love it.*

"Love *this*?!" Ash screamed, suddenly annoyed as hell at her self-righteous bear. "Growling and roaring? Ripping and tearing? Tasting blood? Smelling death? You want me to love *this*?"

Death is nothing but renewal, the path to new life. These men were abusers of life. Killers themselves. Rapists. Thieves. Sadists. You are good inside, and our in-

stincts will not let us kill those who are good. You must learn to trust me, to trust us, to trust yourself, the bear replied. Then a long internal pause, and the bear spoke again:*And to trust him. He is your mate. He will show you the way.*

"The way to hell!" Ash muttered, staring down at her paws and gritting her teeth as she tried to will herself to Change back into human form. But she couldn't do it, and it terrified her to the core. Was she doomed to roam the desert forever, a killer bear always on the hunt? No way. She wanted out. She wanted her old life back. She wanted to get away. Get away from all of this. End it now. Wake up from this nightmare!

She roared in anguish once more, and then she just started to run. Run as fast as she could. Run. Run. Run. She just needed to run. Run away from all of it. From the animal. From herself. From him. Run, Ash. Run.

20

She barely made it over the nearest sand dune before she felt his dark shadow above her, and she looked up and roared for him to get away, to leave her the hell alone.

"Where are you going?" Adam called down to her as he effortlessly glided along, his wings dark gold and shimmering green in the moonlight of the desert night. "Stop. Ash, stop! Stop now!"

Ash just snarled up at him, willing herself to run faster. She could feel her strong haunches flex and open up as she bounded across the sand. She was still animal, the human inside her still feeling disgust and horror at what she'd done. But something was changing in her mood as she ran, and she couldn't fight it. Slowly that feeling grew until she realized it was joy. Pure joy was washing over her, that same feeling she'd gotten when she was riding the dragon, swooping into the fight, feeling the rush of natural, pure energy as her animal did was it was meant to do, born to do, loved to do.

And then suddenly the blood on her teeth tasted sweet like honey, natural like mother's milk. Did a bear in the wild experience a moral dilemma when it hunted for food, killed to protect its cubs, fought to preserve its territory? There was no judgment. There was no planning. There was no thought. It was just instinct. It was just life at its most basic.

Ash felt the exhilaration soar as she kept running, and soon she was laughing as she bounded across the land. She could feel the protective wings of her mate above her, and in that moment she decided she was happy, that she'd never been happier, that maybe there *was* something to this whole animal thing!

Or is that just you losing control of your animal, came the thought from Ash the woman, the human buried inside two tons of fur and muscle. Convincing yourself that what you just did was OK. Convincing yourself that it's OK if you do it again, if you let the beast run wild as and when it sees fit.

"But how do I control it?!" she screamed out loud as the dread returned so quickly it made her choke. "I can't even Change back to a human! How do I control this?! I can't! I just . . ."

"I will control it," came his voice from above her. "I will control your Changes until you learn to do it yourself. I will bring you back to human form when you are not able to do it yourself. I will bring you back by taking you to the place where the human and the animal is always in balance, where the two sides of you are always in harmony, that place where every human is an animal."

Ash felt a ripple go through her body, the energy in her transforming in a way that made her heat rise so fast she growled back at him. She looked up into his eyes, those dragon-eyes shining gold and green, their gaze fixed on her. And as she stared up at him, her legs still churning as she ran, she watched him Change back to human form, Adam's handsome face breaking through as the dragon's wings pulled back in a puff of smoke, his talons turning back to hands and feet, his tail cracking through the air like a whip and then disappearing.

"What the . . ." Ash muttered as she felt herself slow down and then stumble, flying head over heels on the soft sand. She rolled onto her back, wincing as she felt the sand scratch her skin. "Oh, shit, I'm back! How . . ."

But she already knew how. She already knew why. This was what Adam meant by taking her to that place where every human was an animal, where the human and the animal existed in balance, where man and beast were one, just like nature intended.

He was on her before she had a chance to take another breath, his naked body slamming down on top of her as he fell from the sky, a naked, bronzed god who'd lost his powers just so he could have a taste of a human woman. She screamed in shocked delight as he grabbed her wrists and spread her wide beneath him, kissing her ferociously on the mouth before dragging his tongue all over her face, licking her cheeks and neck, her forehead and ears, grunting and growling as his cock pushed against her mound, his hips forcing her legs apart.

"Do you feel it?" he gasped as he came up for air, his body still pinning her down, his eyes burning with the heat of his passion, the fire of his need. "Do you feel how this brings the animal and human back into balance? Do you feel it?"

Ash could barely speak, her heat was so out of control. She bucked her naked hips up into him, moaning out loud as she felt his rock-hard shaft press roughly against her pubic curls, spreading her slit and grinding her clit. Hell yes, she could feel it, and it felt like nothing on Earth. She could feel her animal in the background, retreating and making way for the human. It somehow made complete sense, she thought as she thrashed beneath her mate, moaning again as she felt him reach between them and position his cockhead against the mouth of her vagina, forcing himself in so hard and fast she didn't realize what was happening until she felt him inside.

"Oh, *God!*" she screamed as she felt the lips of her vagina open wide, his massive shaft pressing against her inner walls and pushing them open, his length driving so deep inside her it felt like it was opening new space in her most secret of places. "Oh, God, this is . . . it can't be . . . I just can't even . . ."

She knew she was talking gibberish, and nothing but more gibberish came out when Adam flexed inside her and then started to take her with everything he had, man and beast, animal and human, all of him inside all of her, all the way inside, all the goddamn way.

21

Adam roared in pleasure as he felt her heat from the inside, sensed the primal energy in the way she thrashed beneath him, heard the ecstasy in her voice as she mumbled some gibberish and half-broken sentences.

"Sometimes it can feel like you are broken," he panted against her cheek as he slowed his thrusts down so he could savor her sex, revel in the beauty of their union, two freaks on the dark sands of the open desert. No morals in sight. All their secrets laid bare like their bodies, naked and natural, perfect and pure.

"What?" she muttered, groaning as Adam gently bit her neck and then lowered his head to suck on her nipples. God, they were luscious! Big and dark red, shining in the moonlight like discs. He could taste the sweat on her, smell the woman in her, hear the mating call of the animal in her. He'd never wanted anything as badly as he wanted her, and he almost shouted in anguish that he couldn't just consume her, make her all his!

"When the animal takes over and the human is trapped inside, powerless to stop its rampage," he said, releasing her nipple and kissing her between her breasts. "It can feel like you are broken. Like there are two parts of you that can never become one."

"That *is* what it felt like," Ash said, her eyes going wide before rolling up in her head from the way Adam was moving his hips while kissing her neck and chest. "Oh, God, that feels good. Do that. Shit, that feels good!" She moaned, going quiet as he slurped and sucked, pumped and flexed. "I did feel broken, Adam. I *am* broken."

"No, you're not broken, Ash. You're only just being put together, growing into what you are, waking up to what you were born to be," he whispered, sliding his cock out of her as he ran his tongue down along her naked belly, circling her belly-button and then pushing his face deep into the dark brown curls between her legs. He breathed deep, taking in her feminine scent as his cock yearned to enter her again and just explode inside her depths. But he held back, slowly teasing her wet nether lips with his tongue, pressing her thick thighs firmly into the sand, flicking her clit until she was whimpering and flailing, dangerously close to orgasm.

She came the moment he slid his tongue into her, and he could feel her come all over his face, her wetness squirting from her slit, drenching his mouth and chin. "You taste like honey," he groaned as he licked and swallowed, his need rising, his lust almost out of control, his desire to possess his mate so strong that it almost scared him.

He flipped her over onto her stomach, raising her ass and spanking her hard on each upturned cheek, roaring as she screamed in surprise, shouting as she howled in pleasure. He rubbed her ass and grinned like a madman, taking huge gulping breaths as he saw how her naked rump gleamed and glistened in the silver moonlight. Yes, they were animals just like every human was an animal, and he could feel the animal in him, taste the animal in her. But neither of them was going to Change. He was in control, even though it felt like he was madly out of control. He was in control. Of himself. Of her. Of space and time. Of the past and future.

A feeling of power ripped through Adam as his cock went ramrod straight, its massive head grazing her between her thighs, throbbing as if it had a life of its own, as if it wanted to enter her in every hole, claim her in every way, take her from above and below, in front and behind, again and again until his balls were empty and his body was exhausted.

"What are you doing?" she gasped as Adam spread her buttocks and placed his thumb firmly on her rear pucker. "Oh, God, what are you . . ."

"Shhh," he whispered, his voice tight in his throat as he slowly circled her rim with his thumb. He could feel her thighs and ass tighten, and he spanked her once more with his free hand, making her big beautiful rear shake and tremble in the most exhilarating way. "Stay quiet for a moment, Ash. Just focus on your body. Don't think. No thoughts. Just feeling. Just pure, physical feeling. That is what it's like to be an animal. Instinct and feeling, always living in the physical, in the body, in the flesh. That is the key to controlling the Change, Ash. When the human in you understands what it means to be an animal, then you can go back and forth at your command. Do you understand?"

Adam kept circling her rear pucker with his thumb as he spoke, his other hand stroking her trembling buttocks and tense thighs. He was speaking with supreme confidence, but in a way this was a journey of discovery for him too. He hadn't taken a woman in years, and when it had happened it was nothing like this. It had felt cold, lifeless, without passion, without feeling. It had almost disgusted him, and he'd decided that it was better to be alone than with someone who didn't arouse him, didn't awaken the beast in him. His dragon had protested all the way through that last interlude, which must have been ten years ago.

Your mate will come, his dragon had whispered. *Do not waste our time and energy on meaningless, unsatisfying encounters. Your mate will come. When the time is right, she will come. The universe will bring her to us.*

"And now you're here," Adam whispered as he watched her slowly relax under his controlling touch, a low moan coming from her heaving body as he slipped his fingers between her thighs and felt the wetness coat his hand. "You're here, and it terrifies me. It terrifies me because I know I would do anything to protect you, destroy anyone who threatens you, burn the world to a crisp if anyone tried to come between us. You make me vulnerable, and it terrifies me. It fucking *terrifies* me!"

Yes, but she also makes us more powerful, whispered his dragon.*And the price you pay for that power is the vulnerability that comes with having someone to protect.*

"What power?" Adam muttered. He knew he was talking out loud, but Ash seemed lost in herself. She was doing exactly what he'd told her: To let go of all thought and focus on her body, on her sensations, her pleasure.

But the dragon was silent, and Adam could feel it retreat once more, making way for the man to take his woman, to show her what control meant, what true pleasure felt like, how the body was no less noble than the mind, the animal no less pure than the human.

Adam blinked as a sudden focus came over him, and every muscle in his body tightened as he felt the arousal whip through him like a snake. He stared down at Ash, her curves on full display before him, her arms stretched out, ass upturned, brown hair loose and wild. He yearned to take her, to satisfy his need. But then he grinned as he realized this was an exercise in control for both of them. He needed to hold on for her sake. This was about her, not him. About showing her she could trust him . . . trust him to take her there and back, trust him to help her control her animal, balance the two sides of her, bring body and mind into harmony.

Slowly he pulled his hand out from between her thighs, gasping when he saw how wet she was for him. He raised his dripping hand to his face and smelled her essence, tasted her nectar, pushing all thoughts away as he allowed the animalistic need in him to flow free. Ash was grunting and snorting gently, and Adam could tell she was lost in her body in the most beautiful way. Every inch of her nakedness was now an erogenous zone. He could make her come by touching her anywhere, he was sure of it.

"Spread for me," he whispered, massaging her buttcheeks with his other hand. "Spread for your mate."

She obeyed instantly, instinctively, her back arching down as she spread her thighs and raised her buttocks as high as she could. Adam groaned as he saw her rear hole shining clean and beautiful in the moonlight, and slowly he coated her rim with her own juices as she shuddered from his touch.

His cock was throbbing to enter her rear, but Adam wasn't going to take her there. Not yet. This was about control—control over himself as much as control over her. He smiled tightly as he circled her rim once more and then positioned his middle finger right at her rear entrance. With his other hand he grasped his own balls, groaning out loud when he realized how full and heavy they were, almost like his body was producing more seed now that his mate was here. He moved forward on his knees, bringing the oozing tip of his cock to her exposed slit and holding it there.

Slowly he rubbed his cock against her dark lips, gently opening up her asshole with his wet middle finger as she shuddered, her breathing speeding up, her body moving in rhythm with the circular motion of his fingers.

"What . . . what's happening?" she muttered, turning her head halfway, her eyelids fluttering as if she was coming out of a daze. "What's happening, Adam?"

"We are happening," he whispered. "*We* are happening."

She nodded as if she understood, even though

Adam wasn't sure if he himself understood what he was saying, what he was doing, what was happening. And then all thought was gone from Adam's mind as well, leaving nothing but the physical, nothing but the body, nothing but pure pleasure, the joy of judgment-free release.

He drove his hips forward as his eyes closed, grabbing her hair and pulling her head back. He massaged her neck gently as she moaned, and then, just as he drove the last six inches of his cock into her, he slid two fingers into her mouth and then jammed that middle finger all the way into her ass, entering her simultaneously in three places at once, possessing her completely, absolutely, all the way, all the damned way.

22

She came immediately, the force of her orgasm making her choke as she sucked on his fingers like a hungry beast, clenched her asshole around his finger, tightened her pussy around his massive cock. It felt like she was being taken by three men at once, and her eyes went wide open as she gasped in shock. But then she saw it was just him, her mate, her man. He was taking her everywhere at once, and as her climax rose and fell like waves on the ocean, she saw an imaginary vision of his dragon reveling in the joy of their union, its talons and tail filling every hole as Adam took her.

She growled in pleasure, snorted in shock, groaned in ecstasy as she felt her saliva coat Adam's fingers as she sucked them. The sensation of his finger curled inside her rear canal was sickeningly sweet, and she moved her ass in time with his circular, driving motion. Somewhere inside her a voice whispered that she was sick, twisted, perhaps even disgusting. But that voice was a distant whimper. It carried no authority. Her body was the only authority, and her body was telling her this was beautiful, natural, right as rain, perfect as a puddle.

Ash balanced herself on one arm and reached below her with the other, grasping Adam's heavy balls and holding them in her palm as he roared in pleasure. She smiled as she sucked his fingers and pulled him back and forth from beneath, laughing in mad pleasure as she felt him groan and grunt from the magic of her touch. Soon she was controlling his thrusts with her gentle grip, making him shout in pleasure as she massaged him, clenching her pussy every time she pulled him back into her, her body yearning for his seed.

She could feel her bear inside her, but this time there was no conflict. It wasn't straining to get out. It wasn't fighting for control. It was in ecstasy just like Ash the woman. Things felt like they were in balance, in harmony, in tune with the universe, in line with fate. Meant to be.

He came just as the thought exploded in her mind, her own climax crashing through the ecstasy and making her howl. She bit down on his fingers, tasting his warm blood as his hot seed blasted up into her secret space, filling her warm valley so completely she was overflowing even as Adam pumped more of his semen into her.

He jammed another finger deep into her asshole as he pounded against her rear cushion, roaring so loud Ash wondered if every living creature of the desert could hear them, hear the dragon taking his mate, hear the she-bear squeal in pleasure as she accepted his seed, accepted her fate, accepted . . . herself.

"What the hell did you do to me, you witch?" he groaned, thrusting one last time and then flexing inside her. She could feel his heavy balls tighten in her palm as he squeezed out the last of his load before collapsing on top of her, his weight pressing her face-first into the sand, pushing all the air out of her lungs.

"I don't know," she gasped, giggling at the same time as her climax wound its way down to a steady buzz of pure pleasure. She spat out some sand and gasped again. "But I do know that you're suffocating me. Why are you so heavy?"

"It's mostly my gigantic balls," Adam grunted, and she could feel him grin as he bit her ear gently and then kissed the back of her neck. "They are already producing more seed to fill you with. Give me a minute, and then we will go again."

Ash squealed with laughter, squirming beneath him

as she finally managed to turn and face him. He gave her some space, propping himself up with his muscular arms and looking directly into her eyes. They held the gaze for what must have been a moment, but in his eyes Ash swore she could see forever, a place where time had no meaning, a place where all events unfolded at once. Eternity. Destiny. Fate.

Her mate.

She closed her eyes and let out a slow breath. This was happening too fast. Yes, it felt otherworldly, mystical, magical. But she needed to slow down. Back up. Take a breath and use some goddamn common sense here. What was the end-game? What did she want out of this? A boyfriend who lived in the desert and ate human beings when he turned into a flying monster? A wedding at some stuffy ballroom at the Milwaukee Marriott, her friend Polly dabbing her eyes as Ash swung her big butt down the aisle? Children with this unpredictable killer who'd already taken her twice? Could they even *have* children?! What kind of freaks would those kids turn out to be?! Half-dragon, half-bear?

Dragon-cubs, whispered her bear from the background, and Ash blinked her eyes open and swallowed hard. This wasn't her imagination. This was real. Her goddamn animal was awake and alive. It was inside her. Shit, it *was* her! *Furballs with little wings perhaps. Or gold-and-green bears with talons and scales. May-*

be little dragons with snouts and fur! Mix-and-match!
Scratch-and-sniff!

Ash almost laughed at her bear, and she wanted to answer but stopped herself. She wasn't going down that path yet. Adam already sounded crazy when he muttered to his dragon. What kind of couple would they make if each of them spent half the time whispering to some mysterious "inner voice"? Wasn't that the definition of bat-shit crazy?!

"We are *not* going again," she said firmly, her brown eyes twinkling as she felt his manhood move against her mound. "I don't think my body can take another pounding like that, and honestly, I doubt you've got anything left in those big balls you're so proud of. Damn, Adam, I can still feel you flowing out of me!"

"Well, that's no good," Adam said, frowning as he looked down along their naked bodies. "I will have to pour more of my dragonseed into you. Give me a minute."

He reached down between them, his fingers grazing her naked belly and making her shiver. She raised her head and looked down along her body, smiling as she saw her big breasts hanging off to either side, her nipples red and raw from the way Adam had ravished her like he wanted to damned well eat her up! She was surprised at how comfortable she felt with her body in that moment—in *all* the moments she'd spent with him, actually. It was weird, really. She'd

always been a big girl, and with that came self-consciousness and sometimes even self-hatred. Mirrors
were the enemy. Selfies were carefully engineered to
make her look as thin as possible. But with him she
felt perfectly proportioned, like her body was built
to handle his, her curves designed for his muscle. It
felt natural and free. Like it was all part of a plan.
Meant to be.

Stop it, she told herself as she fought that rising
feeling of connection with him. You're just experiencing some weird form of Stockholm Syndrome
mixed with the release of the natural hormones that
accompany sex. You've been through the most dramatic few days of your entire life, and it's made you
believe there's some magical connection with this
man. Don't lose yourself here, Ash. You still know
nothing about him, about what he's done, what he's
capable of doing. And what you *do* know should be
worrisome, terrifying even!

She gasped as she was suddenly brought back to
the moment, and when she opened her eyes all she
saw was Adam's green-and-gold gaze locked in on
hers. Suddenly she realized that while she was spin-
ning in her head, he'd gently pushed himself back
into her and was gliding back and forth, going again,
just like he'd said.

"Oh, God, Adam!" she groaned as she arched her
neck and felt him flex inside her. "What are you . . .
oh, *God!*"

He came right then, looking deep into her eyes as

his handsome face twisted into a grimace of pure ecstasy. She gasped as she felt him pour another load into her depths, but this time it was smooth, gentle even, like it was just the man and not the animal, another side of him taking her, claiming her, loving her.

He kissed her lips as he finished, and Ash just blinked as her body trembled and shuddered. She knew she was coming too, but it was a gentle, subtle orgasm that flowed through her like slow ripples on a silent lake. She curled her toes and moaned as he kissed her again, and then he pressed his weight down on her once more and they were one, joined together completely.

They stayed like that for what seemed like hours, and then finally Adam raised his body and looked into her eyes.

"You did save the head, didn't you?" he said.

"What?" she said with a frown. "What head?"

"Sheikh Ahmed. We need his head to collect the bounty. I told you to save it."

Ash stared up at this madman who'd just made beautiful love to her and was now asking if she'd saved the head of a man she'd ripped to shreds while under the influence of her bear. OK. Cool. No worries. This is normal, Ash. This is the new normal.

"No, I didn't save his head!" Ash said, pushing against him as she felt her panic rise along with the memories of what she'd done. "Oh, my God! What did I . . . oh, my *God*!"

Adam grunted as he rolled off her and chuckled. He

seemed least concerned about her state of mind, and Ash wanted to slap his smug face. Then she wanted to slap her own fat face for giving a damn about what Adam felt about her state of mind.

"Death is nothing but renewal, and you will need to become comfortable with it," he said in a calm, authoritative voice that just annoyed Ash even more.

"I don't *need* to do anything I don't want to do," she said, frowning as she sat up and looked around for her robe.

Adam snorted. "Ah, feminism. Is that a line from some article in *Cosmo*?"

This time Ash did slap him, hard across the face in a move that came so fast she was shocked at herself. "Oh, shit!" she said, covering her mouth when she saw the anger explode into Adam's eyes, making them blaze in the moonlight as she saw him fight to control himself. "I didn't mean to hit you! I'm so, so sorry!"

Adam was quiet, and Ash felt her breath catch as she watched his chest heave, every muscle on his body tightening as those eyes narrowed to slits. She could see him fight back the rage, and in that moment she understood what it must have taken Adam to control his dragon, what sacrifices Adam the man must have been forced to make over the years. She also understood that he was not to be trifled with, that in the end he was a dragon, and there wasn't a creature in the cosmos that could go up against a dragon and expect to come out unscathed.

"It's all right," he said through gritted teeth. "I suppose I deserved that. I have been outside of modern society for too long."

Ash twisted her mouth and stared in disbelief. "Um, feminism has been a thing in America since like the fifties. Exactly how long have you been out of modern society, Adam?" A chill went through her when she remembered he'd never answered her question about his age. Yeah, he'd spent two years in high-school with her, but thinking back, he didn't really look like a teenager back then, just like he didn't really look like he was in his thirties or forties now. He looked ageless. Like he was stuck in time or something.

Adam didn't answer, instead just reaching out and tossing her robe at her. He sat there naked as she covered herself, and she could see the loneliness come through as he gazed at her. Then he looked away, as if he'd willed himself to stop thinking whatever he was thinking.

"You're fighting this just like I am," she said without thinking.

"Fighting what?"

"This," she said, looking at him and then back down at herself. "Whatever's happening here."

"What is happening here?"

"I mean what just happened," Ash said, her annoyance rising again when she saw how Adam had shut down. "Between us. For the second time."

"You mean sex? You can say the word, you know.

Sex. Intercourse. Fucking. Just like the animals do. Every creature from a mouse to a goddamn whale. Killing. Fucking. Eating. The holy trinity."

Ash stared at his muscular, tattooed back. What the hell had just happened?! How had this man just switched off like that?! An hour ago he was looking lovingly into her eyes as he filled her with his seed, and now he couldn't even look at her?! Was this the classic unfolding of the one-night-stand? Was she about to get ghosted by a freakin' dragon?!

This is between you two humans, said her bear, and Ash swore she felt her animal sigh like it was shaking its furry head. *His dragon knows we are mates just like I do. But sadly the mating ritual for humans is not as simple as it is for animals. So many thoughts. So much consideration given to logic, common sense, society's rules. Nonsense if you ask me. But I am just a dumb bear. Besides, this is amusing to watch. What's next, Miss Feminist Hot-shot Reporter? What comes next?*

Ash almost laughed out loud at her bear, but she managed to hold her firm expression. Shit, the dumb furball was right. The human mating process was complicated as hell, wasn't it? Animals could just sniff around to figure out who was in heat, and then *boom*—done! Scratch-and-sniff indeed!

But the feeling of lightness didn't last long, because Ash knew that despite what her bear wanted, what his dragon wanted, the complexity of the human mating cycle had to be played out. And there was no guarantee that the animals in them would win out. Hell, she wasn't sure if she *wanted* her bear to get its way! What would life with Adam be like? Killing, eating, living in the goddamn desert? What about her career? What about the other things that she cared about, like making a difference in the world, using her talents and intelligence to make things better, to expose injustice and conspiracy, to play a role in sustaining democracy as part of the unbiased free press? Was she going to give it all up for great sex with a loner dragon who was probably gonna ghost her once he got bored of her fat ass?!

Nope, she thought as her jaw tightened. Besides, it would never work long-term between them anyway. Yeah, he'd been joking with that feminism comment, but there was still something dominant and old-world about Adam. She could tell that if they were together, he would always be in charge, always lead, always be the goddamn man. She was a dominant woman herself. She'd always been that way. She'd never be able to yield to a man like that. And she knew he'd never bow down to her either. This was a non-starter. A total non-starter.

So just finish what you started, Ash told herself as her head spun from all the back-and-forth. She didn't know which way was up, what she wanted from this relationship, whether this was even gonna *be* a relationship! Nope, she didn't know which way was up, but she knew which way was forward. The story. Her story.

Ash took a breath as she refocused, thinking back to his last real question. The head. The goddamn head.

"*You* saved the head, didn't you?" she said softly, a smile breaking on her face as she searched her memories and came across the moment when the dragon had pierced the dead Sheikh's head through the eye socket and carried it with them. "The dragon in you wouldn't let you lose the bounty, lose the treasure."

Adam turned halfway, his handsome face lighting up with a smile. "I knew I couldn't trust a bear to keep the head. We're lucky you didn't crush his skull. I don't know if Benson would have accepted some bone fragments and a blood-stained scrap of beard as proof."

"Benson," Ash said. "That's the third time you've mentioned his name. So he's the banker, the handler, the man who pays you to do what you do?"

"I do what I do because it's what I do. Not because someone pays me."

Ash rolled her eyes. "Nice line. It sounds like something from an action-movie made before feminism hit. Now answer my question, please. Who is Benson?"

Adam swallowed hard, hesitating for a moment. "All right. We do need to see him before that head rots anyway. You got questions? Well, Benson usually has the answer. You'll see when we meet him."

23
<u>DUBAI</u>
<u>UNITED ARAB EMIRATES</u>

"We've met before," said John Benson, making no move to shake hands or even rise from his battered leather chair. "You were too young to remember." He turned his attention from Ash to the leakproof plastic bag sitting on his dark teakwood desk, twisting his mouth in amused disgust and then looking up at Adam with a sigh. "And I told you I don't actually need their goddamn heads! This isn't the Wild West in the 1800s! A photograph or short video works fine. Besides, we've got satellites covering almost every inch of desert these days. If I ever doubt your word, I can always track down the video footage and confirm your kill. Though usually I find that you've killed *more* than what you've claimed."

Ash frowned as she studied the distinguished looking man seated before them. She and Adam had flown across the desert, through Iran and Saudi Arabia, landing outside Dubai in the United Arab Emirates. They'd carried a bag with clothes, cash, and a head (carefully wrapped in plastic, at Ash's insistence). These appeared to be the bare necessities as far as Adam was concerned.

"Did you say we've met before?" Ash said, frowning as she tried to remember. She shook her head. "I don't think so."

Benson smiled, the lines around his eyes showing prominently. It was a surprisingly warm smile, and it made Ash think he wasn't as old as he looked. He'd just seen too much with those gray eyes, perhaps.

"It was very brief," he said softly. "You were just a few months old. You wouldn't remember."

"I guess not," Ash said, blinking as she stared into Benson's eyes. "Why were we even in the same room when I was a few months old? Were you my pediatrician?"

Adam snorted from her left. "Doctor Benson. That's a good one. Did you even finish college, John?"

"West Point, and then a PhD from the University

of Virginia," Benson said, a twinkle in his eye as he stayed focused on Ash. "Write that down. It'll add some color to the article."

"What article?" Ash said, glancing at Adam and then back at Benson. Had they spoken before for one of her stories? Had he read her stuff? Been following her career?

"The one that's going to introduce Shifters to the mainstream, confirm the rumors, explain the sightings." He paused and glanced over at Adam. "Explain *him*."

Ash glanced at the dismembered head and chuckled. "Yeah, that would take more than an article. It would take several hundred pages of deeply disturbing psychological analysis."

Benson roared with laughter, thumping his open palm on the desk and making a pen-holder jump in glee. Adam raised an eyebrow and stared at her, but Ash just kept a straight face and shrugged. "What?" she said to Adam, holding back her smile. "It's true. You're a deeply disturbed individual. You carried a man's head here in a Ziploc bag!"

"Technically *you* carried the head," Adam said, eyebrow still raised. "Also, the man in question was killed by—"

She gave him a look that could have stopped traffic, and Adam grinned and pulled an imaginary zip across his dark red lips. Benson, who'd been watching with amusement, turned to Ash, his gray eyes dancing with what Ash swore was delight.

"*You* did this?" he said, poking the head with a plastic pen. "So then the transformation has happened. You've had your first Change." He stared at her, a distant look in his eye. "Which means your parents failed with you too, just like they failed to stop your brother from Changing." He sighed and shook his head. "If only they'd listened to me back then. If only they'd understood that Shifters do have a place in this world. If only . . ." He trailed off, blinking twice and then forcing a smile at Ash. "All right," he said, glancing over at Adam and then back at Ash. "Sit down, both of you."

24

"I prefer to stand," Adam said firmly, crossing his arms over his chest and staring down at Benson. "I won't be staying long. This is between you two."

He felt Ash turn to him, her face lit up with alarm. He didn't look at her. He couldn't look at her. If he did, it might weaken his resolve. He'd decided on the way here that this would be his way out—he'd connect her to Benson and then step out of the story before he got sucked in. After all, Benson was the only hope they had of finding Ash's brother Bart, and Ash could take it from here. Adam's obligation was done. He'd done what he said he'd do. Now it was her story, and he wasn't going to be in it anymore.

His body tightened as he felt Ash's brown eyes bore a hole through him. She hated him in that moment, Adam could tell, and it gave him a perverse satisfaction to feel her anger. Good, he thought as he kept his eyes on Benson even though every other sense was focused on Ash. She looked beautiful in the khaki shirt and black pants that she'd insisted on buying when they'd entered the city of Dubai, even though he'd thought she looked just fine in the white robe through which he could see her nipples whenever he wanted.

His resolve wavered as he felt his cock move at the very thought of Ash naked, her strong hourglass figure bathed in sunlight, her curves glistening in moonlight, her smell awakening the man and the dragon in him all at once . . .

He gritted his teeth and clenched his fist, reminding himself that this was precisely the problem. This woman compromised everything he valued about himself: Discipline, focus, invincibility. He didn't know himself around her. He couldn't control his dragon around her. And he sure as hell couldn't control that instinct to possess and protect her, consequences be damned. If he tried to follow that damned dragon's insistence to take her as his mate, their story was only going to end one way: Tragedy and destruction.

"Suit yourself, Soldier," Benson said, leaning back

on his chair and raising his feet up onto the desk. He glanced over at Ash, gesturing to one of the two empty chairs across from him. "Miss Brown?"

"Yes, I'll sit," Ash said, her jaw tight, her face red with what Adam could tell was a mixture of panic, anger, and . . . determination?

He studied her face in profile, blinking away the annoying thoughts of how beautiful their children would be, little critters with Ash's eyes, her hair, her strength. It took some effort to force those thoughts away, push that pesky dragon's whispers into the background, and when he managed to regain control of his mind, Benson was already talking up a storm.

". . . but they meant well," he was saying. "They only wanted to protect you and Bart, to give their children a shot at a normal life."

Ash was now riveted by what Benson was telling her, and Adam stared at the veteran CIA man and frowned. He trusted Benson with his life, but the man had a way of keeping secrets, withholding information until it was relevant, until he could use it to get what he wanted. He was an honorable man, a patriot to America and deeply committed to seeking justice all over the world; but Benson was a wily old fox too. He had to be. After all, he played the game with the best of them—and the worst. What was his game here?

"Normal?" Ash shot back at Benson. "They were

gone from my life by the time I was seven! Bart was already missing by then! Was that their plan?!"

"Their plan was to cure you and Bart of what they believed was a disease, a mutation, a sickness," Benson said softly. "Being Shifters had brought nothing but violence and misery to their lives, and they didn't want that for their children." He took a breath, shooting a look at Adam before turning back to Ash. "But we can't change who we are. We can't fight what's inside us. One way or another, it's gonna come out."

Ash was breathing hard as she processed what Benson was telling her. "I do remember my parents giving me injections when I was a kid. They said it was vitamins or something. And you're saying . . . what are you saying? That my parents were bear-shifters and they hated what they were? That they'd developed some drug to . . . to *cure* what they believed was a disease?! I don't believe that. I can't believe that!"

Benson took a breath, his face softening. "I'm saying that your parents loved you, and they did what they thought was right. It happened to turn out that they were wrong, and it cost them everything."

Ash closed her eyes tight, her lips trembling, her head shaking. Adam frowned as he listened to Benson. He hadn't expected any of this from Benson, but he wasn't surprised. He knew Benson had recruited Bart the Bear early on, and so he must have known Bart and Ash's parents.

"My parents . . ." Ash said, her voice a low whisper. "What happened to them? My aunt and uncle just told me they were killed in the line of duty. They got military burials. The flags, the salutes, the whole deal. When I was in college I tracked down all the reports I could find, and they were pretty generic. Killed during a routine procedure, details classified. What happened, Benson?"

"Your aunt and uncle raised you," Benson said slowly rubbing his gray beard. "But they aren't Shifters, are they?"

Ash snorted, raising her arms to the side. "How the hell should I know? I didn't even know my parents were Shifters! I didn't even know *I* was a Shifter until . . ." She trailed off, her eyes darting towards Adam as he listened quietly, wondering if he could make a dash for the door before he got pulled into the building drama. He could feel his dragon chuckling in the background like it was loving this, loving how the human had to deal with drama while the beast simply did what the hell it wanted, when it wanted.

"Until you met Adam," Benson said, his voice still soft and low. "Yes, I saw the footage from Bosco's Coffee and Cake. Quite a dramatic first date. But inevitable. Unavoidable. Meant to be."

Adam buried his face in his hands and groaned. "No," he muttered. "John, do not even go there. I'm not listening to this shit."

"Fated mates," said Benson, his gaze moving to

Adam. "I've said it before, and I'm saying it again. It's part of the transformation process, part of a Shifter's evolution."

"Oh, and you're some goddamn expert in Shifters and their freakin'*evolution*? Is that what your PhD is in?" Adam snarled, his fist clenched so tight he thought he might draw blood.

"Arabian History and Middle Eastern Studies," Benson said with a wink at Ash. "With a side-interest in Shifter matchmaking."

Ash snorted as Adam groaned again. He ran his fingers through his thick black hair as he tried to control his emotions. For a moment he wondered if he should just call forth the dragon, blow the walls wide open, blast through the roof of this nondescript CIA safehouse in Dubai. To hell with all of it. Everything was unraveling, so maybe he should just help it along. Just give in to the animal, just like Bart had done. What was anyone gonna do to him anyway? They couldn't shoot him, burn him, or even freakin' catch him! He could rule the goddamn world with fire and talon!

Adam almost choked as he felt the dragon surge inside him, visions of power flooding his mind's eye as he felt the energy flow through him. Energy that scared him. Energy that was different from what he'd felt from his dragon before. Was Benson right? Was there another transformation happening? Was his dragon *evolving*?

Once again he looked over at Ash, and when he

rested his gaze on her pretty round face he immediately felt that surging energy settle to a steady buzz. He blinked as he tried to understand it, understand himself, understand what Benson was talking about. The man wasn't a Shifter, but he'd actually known more Shifters than Adam had! He'd brought Adam the dragon, Bart the Bear, and Caleb the Wolf together. Yeah, the experiment had blown up in his face, but it was a good idea. Or at least an honorable one. Benson wanted to use the Shifters and their powers, sure. But he also wanted to give them a place in the world, give them a cause, a purpose, a way to channel that animal aggression . . . a way to help them find the balance between human and beast. He actually gave a damn, and that counted for something. No one had ever given a damn. And now he was in a room with not one but two people that might actually care. Was he really going to turn around and walk away?

Yes. Because caring makes you weak. Love makes you vulnerable. Vulnerability means you've given up control to someone else, someone who has a hold on you. It means you've lost control, and to lose control means fire, destruction, and death. He had to walk away. There was no choice. Enough of this bullshit about—

"Fated mates," Ash said, glancing over at Adam and then back at Benson. "You mean two Shifters that are meant to be with one another. That's the entire basis of the paranormal romance industry, you know."

Benson laughed, his gray eyes shining as he studied Ash's glowing round face. "Doesn't have to be two Shifters," he said. "A Shifter's fated mate could also be a human. But in my experience, it usually turns out to be two Shifters." His gaze darted from Ash to Adam and back again, those gray eyes of his twinkling brighter. "Sometimes it takes a while for the connection to be made. But there's no stopping it. No running from it. No hiding from it. It's what brings balance to the human and the animal, and I think it's what will bring balance to the world at large."

Adam burst into scornful laughter, clapping his hands once as he laughed again. "Balance to the *world*?! Good God, John. You've lost it, haven't you? Too many years sitting behind that desk. Maybe you've even been reading some of those romance novels. Happily ever after and all that crap. You know better than that!" Adam's laughter faded, his lips locking into a scornful twist. "At least you did know better than that."

Ash ignored his outburst, blinking and keeping her focus on Benson. "What do you mean by that? Balance to the world?"

Benson sighed, looking down at the papers and paraphernalia on his broad desk. "I'm not sure yet, to be honest. I see it in terms of evolution, of life and nature finding a way to bring things back into balance.

I don't know how long Shifters have existed, but I do know that more and more are coming out of the woodwork, waking up, their animals coming to the forefront. I think the Shifter gene has been mostly dormant for centuries, passed down through certain bloodlines such as yours and Bart's, Adam's, Caleb the Wolf's, and a few others that I've come across in the military." He smiled. "Actually, a lot of Shifters seem drawn to the military. And that's what gave me hope to begin with."

"Hope for what?" Ash said, leaning forward. Adam could feel the excitement in her, see it in her expression. It was contagious, and although he still wanted to get the hell out of here, he felt his own curiosity rising. Damn this woman! She was infecting him with her childlike innocence and annoyingly upbeat curiosity! "Tell me! Tell me!"

Benson laughed again, glancing up at Adam and then back at Ash. "Hope that there is an instinctual need for Shifters to find balance, to give their animals an outlet for the natural aggression and energy while overlaying it with a sense of purpose and discipline. And the military is all about discipline and purpose. So yeah, I think the Shifter genes are becoming active because the world needs their power. Maybe it's nature, evolution, the Gods and Goddesses sending help in a time of violence and chaos . . . whatever explanation works for you."

Adam crossed his arms over his chest and let out a loud sigh of utter disdain. "And you're the chosen one who's going to help us wake up, channel our powers, control our animals? The wise old wizard, right?"

"Something like that, yes," Benson shot back, his smile disappearing as his eyes went cold like ice. Now Adam saw the old Benson in those eyes, a man who'd made tough decisions, sent men and women to their deaths in the interest of what was right, wheeled and dealed with the worst characters humankind had to offer. He wasn't a Shifter, but he was powerful. He wasn't a wizard, but hell yeah he was wise.

Ash giggled just as Adam felt his anger rise up, and somehow he managed to swallow the caustic remark that almost exploded out of him. He'd heard this shit from Benson before—back when John had put the three Shifters together as a Black Ops crew that would someday grow into an underground Shifter army that would save the world. Or some crap like that. Nice dream. Too bad reality didn't match up with the dream.

Reality never matches up with the dream, Adam thought as he felt his dragon serve up dreamy images of Ash as if it was messing with him from the background. Images of Ash naked and beautiful, curvy and pregnant with his children, Adam flying through the skies with his brood clinging to his broad, scaly back, his massive wings protecting them as they squealed and howled in delight. That wasn't going to happen. A nice dream, but that could never be his reality. Walk away, Adam. Walk away now.

He felt himself turn towards the door, blinking as he felt the dragon thrash and rumble inside him. It was scared, he could tell. It was scared that Adam was really going to walk away from this, walk away from her. Good, Adam thought. That means the human is winning. Adam the man is back in control.

"Going somewhere?" came Benson's voice, but Adam didn't turn as he reached for the doorknob. He could feel Ash's eyes burning two holes in his back, but he still didn't turn.

"The bounty for Ahmed will be deposited in my bank account, I trust?" Adam finally said, still with his back to Benson and Ash.

"Yes," said Benson after a pause. "As always. I get my head. You get your gold."

"Actually," came Ash's voice, and Adam froze when he heard the playfully firm tone, "the bounty is mine. I actually killed the target, and so the bounty is mine."

Adam growled out loud as he whipped around, his dragon rising in him at the very suggestion of being deprived of its gold. Those ancient drives to possess wealth, to seek out and hoard treasure, to revel in the shine of gold and the twinkle of diamonds were alive and well in the simple-minded winged beast, and Adam gritted his teeth as he tried to hold back the need to grab that woman and show her whom she was messing with.

"Careful," he muttered through gritted teeth, and he could feel his canines digging into the inside of his lips. The dragon was yearning to burst free, to discipline its mate, to remind her that you don't come between a dragon and its treasure. "Be very careful here. You don't know what you're doing, Ash."

"I know what *you're* doing," Benson said, cutting into the conversation. "You're turning your back on your duty, your obligation, your purpose in life. You're never going to find happiness out there alone in the skies, Adam. Not anymore. Things have changed, and you damned well know it."

"Nothing has changed," Adam growled. "There was a momentary loss of control in that Milwaukee incident. And I'm walking away from the source of that weakness. That's the right thing to do. The safe thing to do. You saw what I did to those planes, John. Yeah, the pilots ejected in time, but the truth is I didn't give a shit. I would have burned them along with their planes, and you know it."

"Of course I know it. Why do you think I gave the order for them to eject the moment I realized you were out of control, your dragon had taken over, that you were protecting your fated mate and no one stood a chance against you."

"So I was right," came Ash's voice as Adam stiffened, his back still to the other two. She paused, and Adam could feel the triumph in her voice. "You sent those planes to escort Adam away from the city. Technically you weren't deploying them for combat."

Adam heard Benson shift in his chair, and he could tell that John was looking over at him. Still Adam didn't turn.

"Yes," said Benson. "Adam was one of the best pilots in the Air Force. He loved to fly. I thought seeing those planes would calm him down, remind him that he was still a Flyboy at heart. Then I saw the footage from Bosco's, saw him carrying you out. That's when I knew everything had changed."

"What do you mean?" Ash asked. "What's changed?"

"Well, *you* changed, for one," Benson said. "And the way Adam's dragon reacted means you are his fated mate. Which in turn means things are speeding up. Shifters are waking up, and so are their mates. The universe is drawing them together, and that's only going to keep happening."

Adam groaned. "Again with that fated mates bullshit. Can we stop, please?"

"No, please go on," said Ash. "Besides, I thought you were leaving," she called over to Adam, her tone almost taunting him.

"Not without my bounty," Adam said, finally turning and looking down at Ash. She was messing with him, and he wasn't going to take it.

"It's my bounty," she said, her brown eyes narrowing at him, her red lips twisted in a taunting smile.

"Go find another head to put in your little baggies. What a fun and purposeful life. Your parents must be very proud."

Adam roared as he felt himself lose control. He leapt across the room in a flash, knocking Ash's chair over backwards as she screamed in shock. A moment later his hands were around her throat, his eyes wide with madness. But he hadn't Changed. His dragon hadn't come forth. It didn't want anything to do with this outburst. This was the human in him losing control.

Adam blinked as he loosened his grip on her throat, backing up off her and staring in shock. Benson had jumped out of his chair, and Ash was gasping for breath beneath him.

"Oh, shit," he muttered. "I . . . I'm sorry."

Ash stared up at him as she rubbed her throat and caught her breath. "It's all right. I'm all right, I think." She sat up slowly. "Touchy subject, huh? Your parents?"

Benson let out a sharp breath, his eyes wide with surprise as he stared at Ash. "Wow," he said, glancing over at Adam. "A few days together and already she knows exactly which buttons to push. How can this *not* be fated!"

"Shut up," Adam grunted, helping Ash to her feet as he stared at the finger marks on her neck. "Ash, I . . . I'm . . ."

"I said it's all right," Ash said quickly. "I want to hear the rest of this."

"I don't," said Adam, looking down at his hands

as a chill ran through him. First he'd lost control of the dragon, and now he was losing control of the human?! How could this ever end well?! He needed to get out! "This man is a politician as much as he is a soldier, Ash. He'll say what he needs to say so he can get what he wants from you, from us. You can stay here at your own risk."

"You were the one who brought me here," Ash said, raising an eyebrow and crossing her arms beneath her breasts. Shit, she looked so damned hot from above. God, he wanted her!

"Yes, and by doing so I've kept my word. He's the only one who can help you find your brother, and when you find Bart, you'll get the rest of your story. Congratulations on your future Pulitzer Prize for Journalism. Maybe a book deal too. Make sure you describe me as handsome and magnificent. I'm outta here."

"Was that the deal you two struck?" said Benson, rubbing his smooth jawline. "That you'd help Ash find her brother?"

Adam took a breath and nodded. "It seemed like the right thing to do. Bart can tell her more about her family, about her history, about what she is."

Benson shook his head, reaching for his phone and tapping on it. "Yeah, I don't think so. Take a look. This footage is from last week."

Ash's face went pale as Benson turned the phone around and played the video. Adam felt a chill too when he saw what Benson was talking about.

"Goddamn it to hell," Adam muttered as he watched the grainy nighttime footage of a massive grizzly running wild through what appeared to be a village somewhere in South America. He knew it was Bart, but shit, that beast had grown since he'd last seen him. Its fur was matted with dark streaks, mud from the river banks, leaves and twigs stuck in the fur like camouflage. Immediately Adam understood that it meant Bart hadn't Shifted back to a human in a while, that he'd been lost to his animal in the worst possible way. He'd gone feral, wild, goddamn insane.

"This has been going on for months," said Benson softly. "He's all bear now. All beast. The local authorities have already sent out hunters to take him out. None of them were ever seen again. They're going to send in their military to put him down now. And they might actually succeed."

"No!" Ash shrieked, looking up at Adam, panic in her eyes. "Adam, we can't let that happen. *You* can't let that happen!"

Adam closed his eyes as the image of that door began to fade. How the hell was he supposed to walk away now? Ash needed him. Bart needed him. Shit, he was getting pulled into this story, getting deeper into the quicksand of human drama, of responsibilities to the world. Why had he ever replied to that damned email?!

"There's nothing we can do," he said slowly. "He's gone feral. Lost control of the bear. He hasn't been a human in weeks, maybe months, perhaps even longer. The only thing I can do is put him down so he doesn't kill anyone else. And I can't put him down. I won't. As pissed as I am with the asshole for losing control, I'm not putting down a military brother. Benson can clean up his own damned mess."

"*You're* the goddamn mess!" Ash screamed, her face red with fury. "Run, hide, turn your back! That's your entire damned life in five words, Adam! You're pathetic! I don't even *want* to carry your children!"

Adam took two steps back as the weight of her words slammed against his chest. Where the hell did that last line come from?! It only meant that she'd been thinking about carrying his babies, giving birth to their children! Had she been seeing the same images he had? Images of the two of them as mates, parents to little Shifter babies, dragons and bears and everything in between? Was that a sign that maybe, just maybe . . . no, stop that sentimental crap! That life isn't an option, and you damned well know it!

"There is another option," came Benson's smooth voice, cutting through the tension between Adam and Ash. Adam was startled, wondering if he'd been talking out loud. So many years of talking to himself, talking to his dragon, talking to the desert wind, the blazing sun. Maybe he'd lost it. Maybe it was only a matter of time before Benson would be showing footage of the dragon to someone else, calling out the Flyboys and telling them to put him down with extreme prejudice.

But Benson wasn't responding to Adam's inner monologue. He was talking about Bart the Bear, the feral furball whose sister Adam was banging. Could there be a more stereotypical setup for a cheesy romance story? Adam almost laughed as he wondered what Bart the human might say if he knew Adam was screwing his little sis! That would be another story on its own!

"What's the option?" Ash said, still glaring at Adam with a mix of anger and a whole lot of embarrassment for what she'd said about carrying his babies. There was also a hint of pleading in her brown eyes, and Adam felt himself melting like butter in the desert sun.

"Yeah, what's the option, Wizard?" Adam said to Benson, realizing it was the only way to divert the conversation so his thoughts wouldn't drive him crazy.

"If my theory about fated mates is correct, then Bart has a fated mate. She's already born. Already on a path to collide with him. She exists somewhere, and the universe is bringing them together," said Benson softly, his gray eyes moving between Ash and Adam like he wanted to say something more but was holding back.

"Well, good," Adam said, rolling his eyes. "Then the universe will take care of it. I don't need to be involved. All's well that ends well."

Benson smiled, shaking his head and glancing over at Ash. "You see what I had to deal with in that secret task force? A leader who refuses to lead. An Alpha who wants to reject his calling. A king who wants to toss away his crown, turn his back on the throne."

Adam frowned as he stared into Benson's eyes. What the hell was he talking about? John's words reminded Adam of what he'd thought a couple of days ago, the scathing guilt he'd felt about turning his back on Bart and Caleb, his brothers, his goddamn crew.

"Sometimes responsibility is a heavy burden when you aren't prepared," Ash said, and Adam blinked as he stared at this woman talking as if she knew him. Who the hell did she think she was?!

Your queen, you moron, whispered his dragon, finally speaking after sitting there in the background like a smug little reptile. *The universe has put you two together, and the more you fight it, the harder the forces of nature will work to fulfill your destiny. You know she cannot go after Bart alone. You know we cannot let her go after him alone—not after seeing that video. The bear is feral. It would rip its own mother to shreds, it's so damned out of its mind. You're the only one strong enough to control it.*

"Goddamn it!" Adam shouted, not sure if he was talking to the dragon or to Ash and Benson. He decided he was talking to Ash and Benson. "Don't talk about me like I'm not even in the room! All right! I'll go after Bart!" He took a long breath, glancing at Ash, seeing the relief spreading across her face, feeling the joy rising in her breast. "But I go alone. There's no telling what's going to happen. I may not be able to do a thing with Bart. I may need to fight him. Maybe worse. She'd just be a liability, a distraction, in the way."

"Don't talk about me like *I'm* not in the room!" Ash said, her voice sharp and hostile, the strength of her tone making Adam pause. He could see the bear in her eyes, feel the animal in her energy. Something told him he'd need her by his side. Perhaps he'd always need her by his side. "He's my family, and I won't be left out of this. I just won't. Sorry."

"Neither of you is going to be able to do anything with Bart until he's united with his mate," Benson said, once again interjecting. "The best you can do is capture him until his mate arrives on the scene."

"Again with that fate and destiny bullshit," Adam rasped. "So you want us to put Bart in a cage—a nearly impossible task to begin with—and then just sit there and wait until the universe takes its own sweet time bringing his mate onto the scene?"

"The universe always has perfect timing," said Benson. "If Bart has gone feral, it means his mate has already appeared on the scene. It's up to you two to enable the connection. That's part of your duty as Alpha to your crew, Adam."

"So you're saying Bart's already met his mate?" Ash said, shooting a quick glance at Adam.

Benson shrugged. Then he shook his head. "No, or else he'd have claimed her already. It's more likely that one of you two has met his mate. You two are the connection. After all, the universe has to work through people and events to achieve its goals."

"So do you," said Adam, narrowing his eyes at Benson. "You *want* me to go after Bart, don't you. He's a liability, a train-wreck, a goddamn nightmare. You know I'm the only who can put him down, and that's the goal you want to achieve. Cover your own ass just in case this all gets traced back to the honorable John Benson."

Benson just sat back and stared at Adam, not a word emerging from him. Adam didn't believe his own words, but he sure as hell wanted to believe that this was some classic Benson trickery. He felt his mind drifting as Benson's last words echoed in his head. Was it possible the man was right? That it was an Alpha's duty to connect his crew with their mates as well as lead them? That fate and destiny were working their way through Ash and Adam? If so, who was

Bart's mate? Shit, he hadn't met any women other than Ash in years! Who the hell could it—

And then Adam's memory froze on the image of a woman. Dark eyes, brown face, her hair covered in the traditional Arabian *hijab*. A chill ran through him as the memory became clear as day: It was the woman from the group of hostages he'd saved on the very day he'd gotten that email from Ash! The only woman who'd had the courage to jump out from the back of the truck and take over the wheel, driving the rest of the frightened women to safety. Instantly it clicked, and in that instant Adam *knew* the woman would be Bart's mate, just like he *knew* this woman by his side was his own mate. Something was coming together, he could feel it. Like it or not, he was at the center of it. He and his mate. His woman. His queen.

His destiny.

"Goddamn pesky universe," he muttered, letting out a slow breath and shifting his gaze to Ash. "All right," he said to her. "We'll give it a try. But I'm in charge here, got it? You do *exactly* as I say!"

"We'll see," said Ash, standing up and facing him, the heat from her body almost making Adam lose control and take her right then and there. "Are we flying or driving?"

25

Ash smiled as the wind blew back her long golden hair, pressing her big ears flat against her furry head as the dragon slowly glided above the winding Amazon river. Even from a mile up in the air, the river looked massive, its dark blue waters twisting and turning through the rainforest like a knife-wound.

I could get used to this, she thought as she looked down at her large paws, claws hanging on to her drag- on's scales as they flew together. She was scared for her brother, anxious about what they were flying into, terrified by what she'd seen in that video. But right now she felt whole, complete, in tune with something larger that was happening.

"What did Benson mean when he said I knew exactly which buttons to push?" she asked as the drag-on took a slow turn in the air.

She felt the dragon rumble beneath her. "Now's not the time to push my buttons," came Adam's deep dragon-voice. "Last time I checked, bears couldn't fly."

"I flew just fine when I saved your scaly ass from that RPG when we took out Sheikh Ahmed," she teased, digging her claws in just a little harder.

"Oh, so now you admit that we took Ahmed out together. Which means I get at least half the bounty. Actually I should get more, since I did all the heavy lifting in that kill."

"Heavy lifting? Um, excuse me? Did you just call me fat?" Ash said, leaning in and rubbing her snout against the dragon's back.

Adam laughed, the tremor sending shudders through Ash's bear. "I don't think that's even a thing for bears. The bigger the better. The bigger the beautiful."

"The bigger the beautiful? Wow, that's some good grammar. Were you raised by animals?"

But this time Adam didn't laugh, and the dragon made a swift dive that churned Ash's insides. "Not quite," he growled.

"Your parents . . ." she said when she caught her breath. "They weren't both dragons?"

Adam didn't reply, and Ash didn't push it. They flew together for a while, and then finally Adam spoke. "My father was. My mother wasn't, and she paid the price. That's why I stayed away from humans. Humans and Shifters don't mix."

"Shifters *are* humans!" Ash said indignantly. "We're both human and animal, Adam! You know that better than I do. Humans and Shifters will mix just fine!"

"Tell that to my mother," rasped Adam. "We'll stop by her grave sometime and you can talk all you want. You'll understand if she doesn't answer, being dead and all. Though maybe her ghost will talk to you. Who knows."

Ash looked down at her powerful mate. She could feel his pain like it was her own. There was something else there too, though. More than just the pain of losing a parent. There was anger. There was guilt. And there was . . . shame?

"Where is she buried?" she asked softly. "Maybe I *will* visit her grave."

Adam snorted, sending wisps of hot smoke out of the dragon's nostrils. "You'll have to ask my father. He kept her gravesite a secret."

"OK, I'll ask him. Where is he?"

"No idea. Probably dead too," said Adam with a sharpness in his voice. "Good luck finding him."

Ash blinked as she listened to Adam suddenly begin to open up to her about his past. Why now? Had he changed his mind about her? Had he decided he was going to accept that they were together, that she was his mate?

"You forget I'm an investigative reporter. I have

a knack for finding people. And when I do, I'm sure he'll allow his daughter-in-law to pay her respects," she whispered, still teasing but kinda not. She wanted to see how he reacted.

Adam laughed, and his reaction made her laugh too, the sound coming out as a high-pitched roar.

"Oh, so we're getting married? I missed the part where I proposed to you," he said, turning his massive head to the side, his gold eye studying her as it gleamed.

"Fated Shifter mates don't need things like proposals," she said.

"Then we don't need things like weddings either. Weddings cost money. Besides, I don't have any friends I care to invite."

Ash giggled, thinking of Polly and wondering what her best friend would think about being Maid of Honor at a bear-dragon wedding. Then she felt a hint of sadness when she realized that her old life was gone forever. Jokes about bear-claw Sundays aside, Polly would be absolutely terrified if she saw Ash turn into a bear in the kitchen. And could Ash even trust herself around Polly? Could she trust her own animal around someone who wasn't ready to see what nature had created?

Ash looked down at the massive dragon beneath her paws. She knew it was Adam inside the beast, just like the beast was inside Adam. She understood his need to be alone, his need to escape from the judgment of the world, the people running in fear, calling him a monster and a freak.

"You aren't kidding, are you?" she whispered down to him.

"About what?"

"About having no friends. You don't, do you?"

Adam was quiet. Then he turned his head and gazed at her. "You mean buddies who come over on Sundays to watch the game?"

"Something like that. Someone to talk to."

"I have my dragon."

Ash sighed. "You *are* your dragon. It's like talking to yourself."

"Then why do I argue with it so much?"

"Because you're conflicted," Ash said. "You want to reach out to someone, to let someone inside, past your scaly, hard exterior. But you're terrified."

Adam snorted, flashes of light blue flame emerging on his breath. "I am not terrified of anything. I *bring* the terror."

"And that's *exactly* why you're so scared of letting someone get close to you, understand you . . ." Ash paused as the word stuck on her tongue. "Love you."

A rumble went through the dragon's body, and it blasted a streak of red flame into the air. Ash smiled as she felt the heat, knowing it was the dragon's way of saying, "I love you too." Now she just had to get the human to say it.

But Adam was quiet, and although Ash felt exposed

and vulnerable now that she'd said the L word, she decided to hold back. Technically she hadn't actually said, "I love you." She could wait a bit longer. If this was fate, if she was his mate, then what difference did it make *when* he acknowledged that he loved her? Just like it didn't matter who proposed and if there was even a wedding.

But it *does* matter, Ash thought as an image of a strange bear-dragon wedding came to her mind, making her laugh out loud. I'm not just an animal, and not just a human. I'm both, and if this is fate, then I want my wedding! I'm still a girl, dammit! I want to do my hair and my nails, starve myself for a month so I look kinda thin in my wedding pictures, then stuff my face after the cameras have stopped rolling.

"Adam," she said softly. "I want to—"

"There!" said Adam, looking down at some activity in a clearing near the river. They were still so high up that Ash could barely make out the details, but she understood that the dragon could see clearly for miles. "Hold on, Ash."

She dug her claws in just as Adam descended in a steep dive, and the wind screamed past her flattened-down ears as they headed for the action. Ash narrowed her eyes to slits as she tried to see what was happening below, and when things finally came into focus, a wave of panic went through her.

Because there, in a cage made of shining titanium, was a massive grizzly, roaring and howling as it thrashed against the bars, slammed its massive body against its metal prison. It was Bart, her brother. She knew it. She could feel it. He was wild with rage, out of his mind with anger, and as Adam swooped in for a landing, Ash saw the bear's eyes: big and bloodshot, mad and feral. It scared her, and her panic turned to despair as she wondered if there was any hope left for this beast.

"Adam," she said, her voice trembling. "Why is he in a cage? Who could've done this? Why is there no one else around?"

She prepared to jump off Adam's back, to go to her brother. Maybe he'd remember her. After all, he was older. He'd remember his baby sister, wouldn't he? Maybe she could calm him down. Help him through this. Free him.

"No!" commanded Adam, raising a massive wing and slamming Ash on the side, stopping her from jumping off him. "It's a trap, Ash. Stay on me. Stay!"

"No!" Ash screamed, trying to leap off the dragon again. But Adam was too strong, and a moment later he'd taken off again, rising so fast she knew she couldn't jump from this height.

"What are you doing?!" she screamed, digging her claws in as she wondered if she could steer the dragon back down. "That's Bart down there! We need to go to him!"

"Not until we figure out what's going on," Adam

said firmly. "Who put him in that cage? And where are they? No, Ash. This isn't right. It's a trap. I can feel it. I can smell it. I can damned well . . . wait, what's that?"

Ash glanced down, but she didn't see anything. She squinted, and finally she saw movement. A black streak moving around the edges of the clearing. An animal of some kind. Well, it *was* the freakin' rainforest! There were animals everywhere! Why was Adam focusing on this one? What was it, anyway? It wasn't a bear. Wait, was it a . . . a *wolf*?!

"Caleb," came the low, rasping whisper from the dragon, and Ash could feel the heat in its belly as it circled in the air and then dove at such speed she had to use every ounce of her bear's strength just to hang on. "Caleb, you treacherous piece of wolfshit. *Caleb*!"

26

Ash stared into the wolf's eyes as she and Adam flew in at breakneck speed. She had no idea what Adam was planning to do, but she knew that all she could do was hang on and follow his lead. He'd been right: She wasn't prepared for this. As a bear she had instinct and strength. But she didn't have any experience. She was a writer, for God's sake. Adam was a Special Forces soldier. She needed to trust him. Trust her mate. Trust his instincts above even her own.

"Caleb?" she said as she locked eyes with the wolf. Its eyes were blood-red, shining bright like stoplights on a dark night. She couldn't look away, and a strange feeling of dizziness began to wash over her. She felt her grip on Adam's back loosen, and she swore the wolf was somehow controlling her. "Caleb the Wolf Shifter? He's your friend, isn't he? Why is he . . . why am I . . . oh, God, Adam, what's happening?!"

"Witchcraft," roared the dragon. "Caleb has taken in dark magic. Don't look at him, Ash! Do not look into his goddamn eyes!"

But it was too late, and Ash felt the wolf's dark power loosen her final hold on Adam's back. She rolled off the dragon and began to fall, but Adam twisted in the air, shooting a jet of white-hot flame towards the black wolf before swooping in and catching her. He took off back into the skies with her in his powerful arms, the rage still bubbling as he rose so high the air felt cold as ice even on Ash's fur.

"Did you say *witchcraft*?" she finally said once she'd caught her breath. "When did witches become a thing?! Are witches a thing?!"

Adam grunted as he circled high above the scene, his dragonsight peering down. "Ash, we are humans who turn into animals. Yes, witches are a thing. They've always been a thing. I just haven't seen a Shifter fall under a spell like that."

"Wait, Caleb's under a magic spell? Is that what you're saying?"

"Something like that. He's using dark magic. But he doesn't have any witch blood in him, which means he's made a deal with a dark witch or wizard. Or is under their control, become a witch's familiar, a creature that is just an instrument of the witch's dark magic. This is a problem, Ash. A big problem."

"So just burn the problem," Ash snarled, feeling her bear rise up as her black claws clenched and released at the thought of her brother down there in a freakin' cage. "Burn the dog, and I'll rip it apart."

Adam grunted, turning his head halfway and raising an invisible eyebrow. "While I appreciate the sentiment, it isn't that easy. I don't have a lot of experience with witchcraft. I don't know how much power the wolf has. Clearly it has enough to get your out-of-control brother into a cage. It has enough power to knock you off my back."

"What, you scared of a little wolf?" Ash growled. "Well then, just drop me off and I'll take care of it."

Adam laughed, the sound accompanied by a swell of heat in the dragon's belly. "There isn't a witch alive that can stand up to my dragon's fury, I assure you. I'm not scared for myself, Ash."

Ash went silent when she realized he was scared for her, his instinct to protect his mate coming to the forefront. That was why he was flying a mile up in the air instead of planting his massive talons firmly on the ground and facing down that dark wolf, freeing Bart, and ending the game. He didn't want to risk Ash's life and safety. She made him weak. She made him vulnerable. She was a goddamn liability, just like he'd said!

Her mind swirled as she tried to figure out what to do, what to say, how to tell him that she was prepared to handle any risk so long as she was with him, that she felt safe with him, that her bear was strong too. But then the image of that wolf's eyes came back to her, and she knew she wasn't powerful enough to handle whatever was happening here.

Give in to it, whispered her bear just then. *If it's a trap, then become the bait. If whoever is behind this wanted Bart dead, your brother would be dead and not in a cage. So let's get in that cage with Bart. Become the bait, and let your mate follow the trail. The dragon will find us again. Trust him. Trust him even if he does not trust himself fully yet.*

Ash frowned as she listened to her bear. The beast was smart, she realized. Not a dumb furball at all. The plan was risky, but it made sense. The wolf had focused its magic on her, not Adam. Perhaps it knew its magic wouldn't work on Adam? Perhaps there was something else going on? Perhaps she herself was already under a spell? Perhaps she was the target? So many questions. What would an investigative journalist do? Step back and take pictures from a hundred feet away? Or dive in and figure it out?

"Do you trust me?" she whispered to Adam as he circled again.

"What?"

"Do you trust me. It's a simple question."

"Ash, this isn't the time."

"This is *exactly* the time. That's my brother down there. My family. He's in a cage, and your ex-military buddy has put him there. You don't know what's going on, and neither do I. You can swoop in and burn everything to the ground, sure. Maybe that wins the day. Maybe we free Bart. But we don't get any wiser. We won't know who's behind this. We'll be vulnerable to another trap, more dark magic, more witchcraft."

"So what do you want to do? Interview Caleb? Have a nice sit-down conversation with a wolf Shifter who's under a spell of dark magic?"

"Something like that. Do you trust me?"

"Not really," Adam retorted. "Not when it comes to something like this. You have no idea what kind of power exists in the world, Ash. Dark power. Dangerous power."

"And the two of us wield some of that power, don't we? Dark and dangerous?"

Adam rumbled heat through his dragon as he turned again in the air, looking down on the shining cage far below them where Bart the Bear was going insane in captivity—or more insane than he already was.

"We have some power, yes," he growled, and Ash could feel the fury bubble up in him. She knew he could and would burn it all down, fry Caleb the Wolf like a sausage link, melt the titanium bars of the cage, probably burn half the damned rainforest down along with it! Hell, he might burn Bart too while he was at it! No. She had to step in. She had to follow her gut, her instincts, her intuition. And her intuition told her this operation needed her finesse along with the dragon's fury.

She looked down at Adam as a strange feeling of warmth came over her. Suddenly she knew this would work. He would find her. He would find her again. He was her mate, and he would find her like a river finds the ocean, like the rain finds the earth, like those blind baby sea-turtles know which way to run to get home. He would find her.

And so as the dragon swooped low over the trees, Ash leaned forward and kissed Adam's neck. "Come for me, my love. Don't take too long."

Then she leapt off his back, paws out wide, terror and excitement coursing through her Shifter veins, a feeling of love and connection in her heart.

27

Adam roared as he felt her weight leave his back, saw her golden fur flash in the waning light as she leapt off him and crashed into the rainforest below. His mighty heart almost exploded as he realized what she was doing, and he had to twist in the air and direct the scorching flame of his dragon upwards as the fury of losing its mate threatened to drive it over the edge.

"Get a hold of yourself!" Adam roared as he spewed fire and ash up at the skies before getting his dragon under control and turning toward the scene below.

Burn it all, rasped the dragon. *Caleb, Bart, and the entire goddamn rainforest. The wolf has turned to dark magic. The bear has gone feral. They cannot be saved.*

They do not matter. Only she matters. Only our mate matters. Burn them all and get her back!

Adam clenched his entire body, talon to tail, as he controlled the rage of the dragon. This wasn't the time to burn everything down. It also wasn't the time to question what was now obvious to him: Ash was his mate, and the connection was deep and primal, perhaps even magical. If he was worried that he'd never find peace with her, it was clear that he'd also never find peace without her.

"You crazy, dumb, beautiful bear of a woman," he shouted as he narrowed his eyes and frantically searched for Ash. He knew why she'd jumped. At first he'd thought that the wolf's dark magic had taken hold when it looked into Ash's eyes. But then when she'd kissed his neck and whispered that she loved him he knew that the magic hadn't affected her. She'd jumped because she was a reckless, courageous, head-strong woman, not because she was under a spell! It was a leap of faith. If Bart had been the bait to draw them in, she was now a tracking device that would lead Adam to the source, to the ringleader, the puppet-master. Although he hated to admit it, it was a goddamn brilliant idea. Stupid, reckless, and danger-ous, yes—but brilliant. Still, he'd discipline her for this. Spank her beautiful bottom until she promised to never leap off his back without permission again.

He could see the broken branches from where she'd

landed, her shape creating a bear-sized hole in the poor tree. Then he saw Ash down near her brother's cage, the two bears face to face. Caleb the wolf was nowhere to be seen, and Adam hesitated as he circled in the air, watching brother and sister meet for the first time as bears. He watched the treeline for any signs of Caleb or anyone else, but there was nothing.

Then, just as Adam turned his attention back to Ash and Bart, he saw a dark flash. It was Caleb the wolf, but he was moving faster than Adam had ever seen a wolf Shifter move. He was a blur of black fur, and as Adam watched with rising fear, the wolf circled the two bears three times counter-clockwise, its path leaving a streak of dark light.

And then, just like that, all three of them vanished.

Bear, mate, and wolf.

Poof.

Gone.

28

Ash lost all sense of time and space as the wolf circled around them so fast she could barely make out its shape. Then there was a flash of what seemed like dark light, so dense and black it seemed to suck the light out of the setting sun itself. She knew she was being transported, but not in the flesh. She couldn't understand it, but she couldn't fight it either. It felt like she'd been turned into air, dust, dandelion spores floating in the breeze. She wondered if she'd been split apart, if she'd ever be put together again, if this was the end of her story.

So close to a happy ending, came the strange thought as she dreamily went along with what was happening. But now I'm dead. Oh well, I guess it wasn't meant to be. Maybe there's an afterlife where Adam and I will be together. Sure. Why not. We've got Shifters and witches, magic and madness. An afterlife seems logical. What a story that would make! I wonder if my iPhone will work in the afterlife so I can get some pictures to go along with the article!

"You are not dead yet," came a voice through her daydream—or was it an hallucination? "Nor will you be—at least not for a while. I would not kill the woman who is carrying my grandchildren. I am curious to see what kind of abhorrent monsters will emerge from the unnatural coupling between you and my son."

Ash blinked as reality came crashing in so hard it almost knocked her on her ass. Then she realized she was indeed sitting on her ass. On her big human ass, in a shining cage, and—since she'd somehow Changed back to a human while being transported through space and time by witchcraft (it seemed—how the hell should she know!)—she was in fact *naked* on her ass!

"Cover up your nakedness, please. I am not that sort of villain," came the voice again. It sounded old, deep, disdainful. Accented in a way she couldn't place: Maybe a mixture of Middle-Eastern and European. Hard to tell.

Ash blinked again as she felt soft cloth land on her

bare thighs. It was a robe of soft, white muslin, light as a feather, infused with fragrant oils that smelled of sandalwood and desert sage. It was a smell she'd vaguely picked up on Adam when she'd first met him, and she twisted her face in confusion as she examined her surroundings.

Her brother Bart was nowhere to be seen. She wasn't in the same cage as he—hers wasn't made of titanium. She couldn't actually tell what it was made of, but the bars were shining like gold that was somehow infused with energy. Or magic.

She was in a vast, sprawling chamber with red sandstone floors and dark yellow walls. There were open balconies at either end of the room, and from the smell of the air she knew she was back in the desert. If it was magic that had transported her from the South American rainforest, it was certainly powerful magic. Though maybe it took the same amount of magic to teleport someone two blocks as it did to transfer them two continents. Who knew.

"Who are you?" she said, finally focusing on the tall, slender figure standing off to the side of her cage. The man was hunched but wiry, with long gray hair and a thick, dark beard that was streaked with red henna dye. His words came back to her when she looked into his eyes: Eyes that shined gold. Gold like Adam's left eye. "Oh, shit, you're . . . you're Adam's father!"

"Excellent deduction," said the man, clapping slowly like he was mocking her. "Especially after I mentioned you were carrying my grandchildren and I was curious to see what kind of horrible creatures would result from my errant son knocking up a bear-Shifter."

"What . . . why . . . how . . ." Ash mumbled, looking down at her closely clipped fingernails and trying to will herself to Change back into that bear. But it wasn't happening. She couldn't find her animal. What the hell was going on?

"The cage will stop you from Changing," said the man, glancing off to the left, where a dark purple curtain of thick velvet sealed off another part of the room. "A wonderful creation by one of my associates. So useful to control you freaks from Shifting into a mindless beast and running wild. I find it is more relaxing to converse with someone when they are not roaring and trying to destroy everything in sight."

"Oh, you're gonna hear me roar soon," Ash snarled, trying once again to call her bear forth. She could feel it somewhere in the background, but it felt far from her reach, paralyzed, like it was in its own cage. This shit was powerful magic. Damn that witch or wizard behind the velvet curtain. Maybe it was that wolf, Caleb—though Adam had sounded convinced that Caleb had become a witch's familiar, just an instrument for dark magic. "Goddamn it, why can't I Change!"

The man sighed and took a step closer, and only now did Ash notice that his black robe was shimmering just like the bars of her cage. Was he the witch, she wondered. But then she saw those purple velvet curtains move in the background, and she knew someone else was watching. The witch was out there in the background, staying out of the light. Maybe the witch was also a vampire and she'd be burned by the desert sun! Wouldn't that be fun! Maybe she and Adam could roam the earth as awesome vampire hunters!

Stop losing your shit, Ash told herself when she realized she was starting to giggle hysterically as she pulled her robe around her shoulders. You're not dead, and this man clearly wants to talk. At least for now. He's given you a lot of information, so just focus your mind and play his game. You've got some game too, girl. You can verbally spar with the best of them. You've interviewed warlords and concubines, dictators and killers, sleazy politicians and mad scientists. Surely you can handle a conversation with your freakin' father-in-law!

The thought straightened her out, her mind snapping back into focus, her intelligence blazing in like a current of electricity. The first thing her intelligence told her was that since Adam and she weren't married, this black-robed lunatic wasn't actually her father-in-law. Not yet, at least.

"So you're Adam's father," she said slowly. "Nice to meet you finally. He's said *so* much about you. Actually no, wait. He hasn't said shit about you. I just assumed you were dead, because that's what you are to him. Dead. Nothing. Inconsequential."

She threw that out there, carefully watching his expression to see if it had an impact. Nope. Barely a movement on his whiskers. Gold eyes staring straight ahead. Not even a raised eyebrow. This wasn't about some melodramatic yearning to be reunited with his son. This was about something else.

The man shrugged, and beneath his robe she could see that he had the same broad shoulders passed on to Adam. But where Adam was rippling with muscles, the father was wiry and slender, his arms looking stiff and tight, like he hadn't stretched them in years, hadn't spread his wings in decades, hadn't . . . oh, shit, that's why his robe was shining with that same magic, wasn't it, Ash thought suddenly. It was because he was using the same magic on himself! He actually*wanted* to stop himself from Changing to a dragon! He *hated* the fact that he was a Shifter!

The realization hit her so suddenly she almost blurted it out, but for some reason she held back. It was information she somehow knew she'd use later, and as any good reporter knows, information has value. It can be a weapon. It can be currency. It can be a bargaining tool. Store that snippet away, Ash, she told herself as she zipped her lips into a tight smile and narrowed her eyes into slits. Play his game. Stall for time. Because you know Adam is out there looking for you. Your mate is coming for you. This was the plan, wasn't it? It was always the plan. You and Adam are a team, and the game is only just starting.

29

It's over, Adam thought as he turned in the air and swooped in low, opening his throat and spewing flame so hot the few remaining trees almost vaporized. He screeched in anguish, his dragon thrashing and twisting with madness, that image of the dark wolf circling Ash haunting it to the last scale.

Everything seemed to come to an end the instant his mate disappeared before his goddamn eyes, and Adam had burned a hundred square miles of rainforest in his fury, his heat even bringing the river close to a boil!

"Where is she?!" he shouted into the night, turning angrily to the moon and sending a futile burst of fire at it. "Where is my *mate*?!"

But the man in the moon just stared back, silent and lifeless, its light a mere reflection of the Father Sun. Adam rose and dove, surveying the burning forest below him as he flew above the scene of his destruction, breathing in the smell of smoke, trying to control the dragon that wanted to burn more, destroy it all, put an end to the world itself in the search for its stolen mate.

For an hour the dragon flew in wild circles, shooting fire at the stars themselves, rising to tremendous heights and then diving at speeds that almost broke the sound barrier. The amount of energy it was spewing was shocking, but soon Adam could feel himself calming down as the dragon burned through some of its rage and fury, giving the human a chance to take the reins, to maybe think a bit.

"This was the plan!" Adam shouted as he spun in the air. "We will find her! She is our mate, which means we are connected through space and time— connected *beyond* space and time! Just calm the hell down, you overgrown alligator!"

Oh, so now you believe, do you? rasped the dragon. *Once you let her go, you realize she is our mate? Nice job, genius. Remind me again why I even bother letting you control me? It appears that you are the dumb beast, not I. We should have just burned the wolf and maybe the bear too. Circle of life. Shit happens.*

"Maybe you're right," said Adam, grinding his teeth and making sparks fly from his maws. "But she was right too. There's a larger pattern unfolding here. Someone knew we were going after Bart, and they got there first so they could use the bear as bait."

Well, when you know someone is using bait, then the smart move is not to take the bait, said the dragon in that annoyingly pedantic tone that made Adam the man wanted to slap the beast upside the head.

But Adam held his tongue, thinking back to what Ash had said. She'd willingly put herself in that position to save her brother. She'd done it with the faith that her instincts as a reporter would keep her alive and help her figure out the puzzle while Adam's power and strength would come to her rescue. They were a team. They had to trust each other. He had to trust that she would keep herself alive until he got to her. But how to get to her?!

The same way we got to her in the first place, whispered the dragon. *Instinct. The primal magnetism that draws fated mates together.*

"Well, good. Now we're talking," said Adam. "So turn on your primal tracking mechanism already. Let's go!"

The dragon sighed, and Adam felt its frustration. He knew it wasn't that simple. This was about the animal and the human working together. Adam the man had to believe in his fate as well, believe in his destiny, believe that Ash was that fate, that mate, that destiny. He closed his eyes as he slowed his flight down to a steady glide, taking long, slow breaths as he tried to steady his furiously beating heart, control the heat roaring through his massive body.

Slowly he felt things come into alignment, and soon he was smiling as he locked into images of Ash's smiling face, round and pretty, glowing like the moon and sun rolled up in one. The image morphed into another one of her, Ash standing in a field, her body turned sideways, her belly full and round with his babies.

The image sent a wave of energy through him, a dominantly protective instinct so strong and fierce he could almost *see* it stretching across the universe like a golden rope, a shimmering connection, pure cosmic energy, a connection that lay at the foundation of all life.

"She is pregnant," Adam muttered, his eyes flicking open with the shock of realization. "She is carrying my children. My blood."

And then Adam felt his dragon silently turn in the air like it was being pulled by that golden rope, following a cosmic trail blazed through space and time by their connection. The heat still burned in his breast, but it was the fire of passion, not rage. The scorching flame of love, not anger. The power of blood and spirit combined in one, just like animal and human were one again as the dragon soared towards the East, towards its mate, its fate, its future.

30

"I have this vision of the future," said the black-robed man, pacing slowly as Ash crouched in her cage and watched. "A future where I command vast armies of you creatures, you freaks of nature that are only fit to be slaves, to be used as instruments of my ambition."

"Well, that's not a very nice thing to say about your son, is it? Besides, have you seen him recently? Good luck turning Adam into a slave," Ash said, her eyes still locked in on his. Now she saw the slightest movement of his eyebrows, and she knew that mentioning Adam by name had made an impact. Good. More information she could use.

The man grunted. "Not all men become slaves

of their own free will. Sometimes you need . . ." He trailed off, his gaze moving to her belly for a moment in a way that made Ash hug herself protectively. "You need . . . collateral. Something of value that will make even a beast bow its head in submission."

Ash blinked as she felt the truth of his words. He'd said it before—that she was pregnant with Adam's seed. She wanted to laugh it off, to bluff and perhaps say she'd never even been touched by Adam. But somehow she knew it was futile. Somehow she knew that Adam's seed had taken, that she was indeed carrying his children, that in fact her pregnancy was the way this man had locked in to their location, tracked them to South America!

Of course, she thought as she glanced at that velvet curtain and then back at Adam's father. If I'm carrying Adam's children, it means that this man has a blood connection with me in a way! Perhaps that's how the witch latched onto me, onto us! Blood is a powerful connection, isn't it?

Yes, she thought, the panic rising for just a moment before breaking and washing over her like a wave of joy. Blood is a powerful connection, and that's how Adam will find me too. Yes, he'll find me, and he'll save me. So just keep talking. Learn as much as you can.

"So you want Adam's children as hostages so you can get Adam to . . . what, lead your army of Shifters in your quest for world domination?" Ash said, raising an eyebrow and twisting her mouth. "Sounds a bit stereotypical for a dark villain, doesn't it?"

"Villain?" said Adam's father, frowning as if he was seriously offended. "My dear, I am protecting the world from creatures like my son. Beasts like you and your brother! Animals like that wolf who now serves me like a faithful little puppy. Half-breed freaks like whatever you will give birth to!"

Ash swallowed her anger as she clenched her fists. It was probably a good thing the magic was holding her back from Changing. It might be kinda awkward to tell Adam that she'd just killed his dad because he was a rude asshole. It might be best if she left that honor for the son himself.

Adam, where are you, she wondered as she took a breath and let the anger subside a bit. She didn't want to give this dickhead the satisfaction of knowing he was getting to her. Soon she was under control, but the insult would stay with her, she knew. Nobody was going to call her children freaks and get away with it. Because Mommy was a freak too. A freak with razor-sharp fangs and claws that could rip through hardwood like it was tissue paper.

"Wait, so you're not gonna be the grandpa who takes the little ones on his lap and tells them stories of the old days?" she said with a smile. "How disappointing."

"Oh, I'll tell them stories. Don't you worry," he said.

"Why don't you tell me a story first, old man," Ash shot back. "Why are you so scared of Changing into what you really are?"

Now the man's expression changed dramatically, his gold eyes blazing with the hint of a fire much darker than she'd seen in Adam. He was a dragon all right. And he'd been fighting his animal his entire life. She could see it on his face, in his eyes. She could sense it in his energy, damned well *smell* it on him!

He took a long, slow breath, and his black robe shone brighter, as if the hidden witch was dialing up the magic just to keep the old man from exploding into his dragon. For a moment Ash was scared—like *really* scared. Scared not so much for herself, but for everyone else who was suddenly part of her life! Her brother! Her unborn children! Even Adam, who probably had no idea what kind of family drama he was about to fly into!

"You know Adam's on his way, don't you?" she said, the words coming before she could stop them.

Again the man flinched, blinking once and then glancing over at that velvet curtain. Ash swore she saw fear in his eyes, like he was afraid of his son, afraid of the rage that Adam would bring with him when he arrived.

"Who's back there?" she shouted, feeling the confidence soar as she somehow sensed Adam was drawing near, her mate was almost there, his shadow protecting her, his mighty wings shielding her, his love giving her strength. "Show yourself, witch!"

The velvet curtain moved, and from the expression on the old man's face, Ash knew somehow things weren't going as planned for them. Did they not expect Adam to find them so soon? Or find them at all? Was he actually near, or was that just wishful thinking?!

She could feel a cloud of despair forming, but then a shadow whipped past the open balcony, and Ash felt a wave of joy when she smelled the familiar smoky scent of Adam's dragon. He was here! Her mate was here! Her man was here! Here to protect his woman, save his unborn children!

"Fry these bastards!" she screamed, slamming herself against her cage as she felt the energy of her bear begin to emerge, the animal straining to break the bonds of the magic spell. "Burn them both, Adam!"

The wall exploded as the dragon burst through sandstone like it was cardboard, its wings smashing through the outer walls of the building, its maws open wide, a laser-focused streak of flame shooting out with supreme control and deadly aim. Ash howled as she felt his presence, and just then her bear exploded to the forefront, smashing through the puny bars of its cage.

Did I just break the spell, she wondered in a flash

of joy as she felt her body expand to that now-familiar bear-shape, her claws emerging like black scimitars from her heavy paws, her head leaning back so she could roar to her mate, revel in their reunion, join in the fun of wreaking havoc on the villains, animal-style!

But when the smoke of Adam's attack cleared, she saw nothing but an empty room. No burned bodies. Nothing at all. Nothing but that velvet curtain, which had somehow remained unburned.

"Sonofabitch!" she screamed, stomping on the flattened bars of her broken cage. "They're gone! They have to be here somewhere! We have to find them, Adam! Them and my brother!"

But the wind was knocked out of her as she spoke, and when she looked down she saw the dragon's mighty fist close around her belly, its talons holding her firmly as Adam flapped its wings and blasted head-first through the other side of the building. She could feel the possessiveness of the dragon, its instinct to protect its mate and children at the forefront. There was going to be no reasoning with him. No arguing. He'd come for her, and he was taking her back.

And so Ash just sighed and relaxed in his strong grip, letting out a slow breath as she glanced down at the ruins of what looked like a castle in the middle of a desert. And as the warm air blew her golden fur back, flattened her ears against her head, she somehow knew that Bart wasn't in that building. That castle was supposed to be her prison, she understood as she replayed the events of the day. Adam's father wanted to keep her there until she gave birth! But he hadn't counted on Adam tracking her down! After all, he'd used dark magic to find her. He had no idea that Adam would be able to find her not with magic but just by following his instinct. Following his heart. Following his love.

"I love you, Adam," she whispered up at him. There was so much to say, so much to tell him, so much to *ask* him . . . but those three words were all that came out. They were all that mattered. *This* was all that mattered: Being together. Joined as one. One team. One love. One couple.

One family.

"I love you too," came Adam's voice through his dragon, and it was all human, all him, all hers. Hers alone. "I love you, Ash. This is real. I tried to deny it, but I can't deny it any longer. Ash, I saw it! I saw you pregnant with our children! I saw a path open up, a connection that took me straight to you! It wasn't magic . . . it was somehow more powerful! It was . . . it was . . ."

"Love," whispered Ash. "It was love, Adam. The strongest force in the universe. Love, pure and simple."

Adam lowered his head and opened his mouth, sending a gentle burst of warm fire down at her as the dragon rose high above the desert, where the air was delightfully cool. She laughed when she felt the warmth and remembered that she was immune to his fire: Perhaps the only thing on Earth immune to his fire!

But then an image of that unburned velvet curtain came back to her, and suddenly the floodgates opened as questions tumbled into her inquisitive reporter's mind. Who was behind that curtain? Where was Bart? Did Adam even know his father was a crazy freakin' villain who wanted an army of Shifter-slaves to take over the world?! Shit, did Adam even know that Daddy was alive?!"

"So what happened in there?" Adam asked as if his mind was running in synch with hers. "I didn't see anyone. Didn't even smell anyone—besides you, of course."

"Wait, I *smell*? What do I smell like?" Ash said, lowering her head and sniffing her furry armpits.

"You smell like my mate," Adam growled. "Speaking of which, I think it's time."

"Time? Time for what?" Ash said, frowning when she realized that they weren't just flying around aimlessly. The dragon was ripping through the skies like it had a mission, a goal, a destination. "Where are we going, Adam?"

"To my lair," he replied nonchalantly.

"Your *lair*? Who calls their home a *lair*, you freak?!" she said, laughing up at his ridiculousness.

"Dragons do. Look. Down below."

Ash looked down, and she gasped when she saw they'd already crossed the desert and were now over what looked like the Caspian Sea, if she remembered her geography right. It was midnight blue, beautiful and serene, its teardrop shape looking like it had been designed by divine fingers.

"OK, I don't have your dragon's eyesight," she said as she squinted. "What am I looking at?"

"Oh, sorry," said Adam, suddenly breaking into a dizzying dive that made Ash squeal in delight. "There. You see it?"

She saw it, and it was magnificent: There amidst the gentle waves of the Caspian Sea was a small island with three perfectly symmetrical mountains covered in lush greenery, beaches of golden sand all around, the blue waters gently lapping at the shoreline.

And on top of the middle mountain sat a sprawling castle made of white stone, its structure highlighted by four soaring towers, one at each corner, the roofs of the towers shining with goldleaf. The center of the castle was a flat terrace the size of three football fields, large enough for the dragon to land—hell, large enough for *twenty* dragons to land!

"Ohmygod, that's *yours*?! You didn't tell me you were . . . that you were . . ."

"Rich?" said Adam, raising a dragonbrow. "I'm a goddamn billionaire, Ash. Dragons hoard wealth, you know. I've invested well for almost two hundred years now. This is just one of many lairs scattered across the world."

"OK, we are *not* calling our home a lair," Ash said as the dragon smoothly landed on the flat roof, letting go of her so she tumbled head-over-heels like a playful bear-cub.

"Oh, so you're moving in already?" came Adam's voice from behind her, and when she turned she gasped to see that he'd Changed back and was calmly walking towards her, naked as the blue skies above them. "I think my father would disapprove of us living in sin like this."

Ash blinked as she got to her feet, gasping when she saw that she'd Changed back to a human and was buck naked herself. But there was no embarrassment, no shame, no self-consciousness. There was however, some confusion.

"Wait, did you just mention your father?"

Adam shrugged, his eyes narrowing as his mouth curled into a hungry smile. One look down along his rippling abdomen and towards his rising manhood told Ash that the blood was quickly heading south of the border, and there was soon going to be no stopping him.

"My father is dead," he said without hesitation, his eyes glazing over as he looked at her heavy breasts, her big red nipples, the dainty V between her legs that was starting to feel awfully wet suddenly. "That was just an expression. Now come here, woman. Come here now. Let me show you how a dragon proposes to his mate."

Ash opened her mouth to say that um, yeah, your Daddy ain't quite dead. But Adam stopped the words with a ferocious kiss that sucked the breath out of her while sending her spiraling up to that place where only he could take her.

And as he pushed her down onto her back, sucking on her breasts until she screamed, driving his hand between her legs and fingering her so hard she almost came all over his arms, she decided that this wasn't the time.

"Did you say the word *proposes*?" she muttered as she felt his stubble against her thighs and gasped as his stiff tongue teased her clit. "I don't hear the words yet."

"I am spelling them out, letter by letter," he mumbled from between her legs.

She squealed as he clamped her thighs down with his strong hands, his tongue beginning to dance on her clit as she bucked her hips and writhed in ecstasy.

"Yes!" she screamed as her climax rode in like a horde of dragons before he'd even spelled out the first word of the proposal. "Yes! Stop already! I can't take it! I'm already coming! Yes! Yes! Oh, god,*yes!*"

31

Yes, Adam thought as he tasted her sweetness on his lips, smelled her essence with every breath, took in her flavor like it was nectar. He swallowed and licked her again as she thrashed under his mouth, her orgasm bringing forth her erotic juices so they flowed down her soft thighs, down along her divine asscrack as he lapped it all up like the beast he was.

Yes, she's mine, he thought as he spelled out the last letter of "Will You Marry Me?" and grinned as she howled "Yes! Yes! Ohgod, *yes*!" for the millionth time. Then he flipped her onto her stomach, raised her magnificent rump, smacked her twice on each buttcheek until he saw his fingers mark her smooth skin. Marked for him. Now and forever.

"Now and forever mine," he muttered as he kissed her rear, parted her globes, and then entered her slit from below, his throbbing cock opening her up for him as she let out a deep, guttural groan. "My mate. My woman. My bear. My wife. My wife, you hear?!"

"Yes," she moaned as he started to pump into her. "Your mate, your woman, your wife. Your wife, Adam. All yours. Just yours. Yours now. Yours forever."

Yours forever.

∞

EPILOGUE

They married at dusk, with the setting sun, the rising moon, and the winking stars as the only witnesses to their shared vows. She wore a ring that Adam selected from one of his castle's treasure vaults: a gigantic diamond that Ash swore would give her back pain if she actually wore it every day. Adam had wanted to fly them both to Europe or America, have a grand official wedding, bring Ash's friend Polly over too. But when Ash finally told him what had happened in that desert castle, what she'd learned about his father, how many unanswered questions still lingered, they'd decided it was better to lay low as they planned their next move.

"Bart, Caleb, the mysterious witch, my mad father," Adam mused as they lay in each others arms after a post-wedding lovemaking session that made the moon blush red and the stars turn silver with shock. "Where do we even begin? I haven't heard from my father in fifty years! I wouldn't even know where to look for him! And we have to find him to find your brother Bart! Where do we start looking?"

Ash took a breath as she rested her head on her husband's broad chest, smiling as she rose and fell with his smooth breathing. She could hear his heart beat strong and hard, and as she listened for her own heart, she realized that it was beating in perfect rhythm with his!

She frowned as she thought back to something John Benson had said to them, and as she heard her heart beat in time with her mate's, she nodded against Adam's bare chest and looked up at him.

"We might not need to find your father or Bart ourselves," she said breathlessly as it suddenly became clear to her. Fated mates. The universe would draw them together, right? It had already happened with her and Adam. Which meant it could happen with Bart too, right? In fact, it *had* to happen with Bart! That was what fate meant, right?

"What do you mean?" Adam said, looking down at her and frowning. "Who's going to find Bart for us? Benson? Hah! We can't trust anyone and anything right now, Ash."

"You're wrong," Ash whispered, tapping on his chest and then taking his hand and placing it over her own heart. "We can trust this."

"Your boobs? I agree. Let me take a closer look," Adam grunted, lowering his face and opening his mouth wide to take her left nipple in.

Ash laughed and pushed his face away. "No, you animal! Just listen. Our hearts. You feel that?"

Adam sighed and finally did what she said. It took a minute, but then he cocked his head and nodded. "They're in time. Perfectly synchronized."

"Fated mates," she said, nodding excitedly. "Benson said that Bart had gone feral because his fated mate was already here, already on the scene, already born and awake. He said that one or both of us might already have met her. So if we find Bart's fated mate, she will lead us to Bart! She has to! The universe will draw them together, just like it pulled us together!"

Adam sighed again, pulling his hand away from her heart and turning onto his back. He looked up at the dark sky and slowly nodded. Ash looked at him, and as she watched his face, she saw him flinch.

"What is it?" she said. "What did you just think of?"

Quickly Adam shook his head. "It's nothing. Probably nothing."

"That means it's something, Adam! What is it?"

"Well," said Adam, propping himself up on an elbow, "the day I got that email from you, my dragon and I had attacked a caravan of insurgents who'd kidnapped a group of Arab women to be used as sex-slaves for their warriors."

Ash frowned as she felt her bear rumble in the background. "I hope you burned them," she whispered before stopping herself and letting him talk.

Adam grinned. "You know I did. Crispy and crunchy, just like my dragon likes 'em."

"Eww. But all right. Go on."

"Well," said Adam, "when I took out the driver of the truck carrying the women, the girls were all scared out of their minds, too scared to do anything but just sit there and scream. There was just this one woman who wasn't afraid. She jumped into the driver's seat, took the wheel, and got the hell out of there. In fact, she probably saved their lives more than I did! My dragon was running wild, and with all that fire being tossed around, I could easily have caused the truck's gas tank to explode!"

Ash nodded slowly as she realized what he was saying. "So this woman . . ." she started to say.

"She looked at me just before driving off," Adam said, his expression taking on the same excitement that Ash was feeling. "She wasn't scared. In fact, I swear she nodded once, like she was thanking me. It was almost like she knew I was a human inside that winged, fire-breathing beast."

"She was a Shifter!" Ash squealed, sitting up straight. "Adam, that's her! It's got to be! Bart's fated mate. Maybe she was just waking up to her animal! Maybe seeing you, her mate's friend, her mate's Alpha, struck a chord in her. Adam, we have to find her! She'll lead us to Bart! We have to find her!"

But Adam just shook his head, and when she saw the faith in his eyes, she knew that he fully believed in fated mates now, in the undeniable force of destiny, the pull of love and connection.

"We won't have to find her," Adam said softly. "I think she'll find us. She was born to be part of our crew. Born to be part of our family. She was born for your brother. Born to save him from himself. Born for the bear, Ash."

"Born for the bear," Ash whispered, smiling as she felt a tremor of excitement run through her body. "I like that. Has a nice ring to it. Like a romance novel or something."

Adam laughed as he kissed her nose. "I should read one of those sometime. Maybe I'd even like it."

∞

FROM ANNABELLE WINTERS

Liking it so far? Adam and Ash have got their happy union, but the *Curves for Shifters* story is only just getting started! Get *Born for the Bear* and *Witch for the Wolf* right now, and ride along with me and thousands of your fellow readers! These are shifters like you've never seen, I promise!

Also, be sure to check out my internationally popular *Curves for Sheikhs* series (UK customers go here). It's got everything you should expect from an Annabelle Winters series: Drama, madness, and over-the-top heat. Oh, and when you join my private list, you'll get exclusive bonus scenes from the Sheikhs series!

Finally, if you liked this book, do consider leaving a short review. They make a world of difference, even if it's just a few quick words.

Love and thanks,
Always and forever.
Anna.
mail@annabellewinters.com